Discard

Good Night, Maman

NORMA FOX MAZER

HarperTrophy®
An Imprint of HarperCollinsPublishers

My grateful thanks to Harry Mazer for assisting me with interviews; to Linda Fox for
sharing her knowledge of Italy; to Scott Scanlon for sharing his knowledge of the Fort Ontario refugees;
and to Rena Block, Dr. Fred Flatau, Charlotte Gal, Elfi Hendell, Ivo Lederer, Dorrit Ostberg,
and Steffi Winters for their generosity in sharing their memories.

Good Night, Maman

Library of Congress Cataloging-in-Publication Data
Mazer, Norma Fox, 1931–
   Good night, Maman / Norma Fox Mazer. — 1st Harper Trophy ed.
      p.   cm.
   Summary: After spending years fleeing from the Nazis in war-torn Europe, twelve-year-old Karin Levi
and her older brother, Marc, find a new home in a refugee camp in Oswego, New York.
   ISBN 0-06-440923-6 (pbk.)
   1. Fort Ontario Emergency Refugee Shelter—Juvenile fiction.   2. Holocaust, Jewish (1939–1945)—
Juvenile fiction.   [1. Holocaust survivors—Fiction.   2. Refugees—Fiction.   3. Fort Ontario Emergency
Refugee Shelter—Fiction.   4. Holocaust, Jewish (1939–1945)—Fiction.   5. Jews—United States—
Fiction.]   I. Title.
PZ7.M47398Go   2001   00-061350
[Fic]—dc21   CIP
                                                                                                   AC

Designed by Lydia D'moch
❖
This work was originally published in 1999 by Harcourt, Inc.
Published by arrangement with Harcourt, Inc.
First Harper Trophy edition, 2001

For the people of Oswego who welcomed the refugees;
for Ruth Gruber, who gave so much and who still does;
and above all, for the 982 souls who came on the
Henry Gibbins *to the United States: for them and all*
who endured the unendurable, and for their children,
and their children's children, world without end...

Part One

FRANCE AND ITALY
1940 – 1944

1

THE VISITOR

MADAME ZETAIN had a visitor down-stairs. Whenever this happened, everything stopped in our attic room, everything went silent. We didn't talk. We didn't move. We didn't sneeze or scratch an itch. We could breathe, but it had better be silent breathing.

As soon as we heard the knock on the door, Maman went to the mattress, I eased myself to the floor, and Marc took his Buddha pose.

The voices murmuring below went on and on. What could they be talking about for so long? Maman said small towns had few secrets. What if Madame was telling the secret of us? Leaning across the table, whispering, *Don't say a word, my friend, but I've got three Jews hidden in this house. Right up there. Right above our heads.* Her friend would gasp and make a terrible face, as if the very thought of Jews made her sick to her stomach.

Marc sat on top of the black trunk like a prince—calm, his legs crossed, his hands loose in his lap. Was he thinking about home? Or girls...or Papa? He said that at times like these, he went into his mind and stayed there.

"It's like taking a trip. Being somewhere else. Do it," he told me.

Fine for him to say, but for me it wasn't so simple. To begin with, *my heart beat like a drum.* I read that in a book, and it was true. Whenever someone came into Madame Zetain's house, my heart beat just like a drum. It was doing it now, as if it were being pounded over and over, always on the same note. Huge thumps that felt as if they'd break open my chest and slam my heart straight through the floor.

It would be just like my heart to be so noisy and stupid.

Papa had called me Na Na Noisemaker—his nonsense name for me ever since I was little. I was always zooming around, making a mess, drawing and singing and talking. If I had no one to talk to, I talked to myself. When Papa came home from work, I'd fling myself at him like an arrow, shouting his name and telling him everything that had happened all day. *Papa.*

Sometimes when I had to be still, when I could do nothing, then that was what I felt. Nothing. But other times, what I felt was...everything. Like now. It came over me like a huge wave, that feeling, my head turning hot as a stove and my breath rushing in and out. In-and-out, in-and-out, in-and-out—*stop!* I pinched myself hard.

Maman lay on the mattress like a log. Like someone dead. *Maman. Open your eyes. Maman!*

I was sure I hadn't even moved my lips, but Marc looked at me and shook his head.

I straightened my back. I would sit like this, utterly still, until Madame's visitor left. For the rest of the day, and all night, too, if necessary. Marc wasn't the only one who knew how to be patient.

That was one of Papa's favorite words. "Patience, Na Na Noisemaker," he'd say. "In time, the grass turns to milk." The first time I heard him say that, I was four years old. Grand-mère explained about cows and their several stomachs and how grass got digested. "Then I'm drinking *grass*?" I had shouted.

Now I understood a lot of things, and not only about cows and milk. I understood about patience. And that Papa, for once, had been wrong. Sometimes it made no difference how much patience you had. All the grass in the world could turn into all the milk in all the milk bottles, and one thing would never change. It would still be true that Papa had been arrested by our own French police and handed over to the Germans.

It was bad to think about this.

All right. I'd tell myself a story, and I'd begin it properly. *Once upon a time...*

Once upon a time there was a girl named Karin Levi. She was ten years old and quite nice and ordinary, like any French schoolgirl. Her brother, Marc, was two years older and skinny as a stick, although once he'd been a plump, plump boy. Karin had never been plump, but when they lived at home her knees were nice and padded. Now they were like two old bony faces, and as for her arms—

The muscles in my legs were cramping again. Marc claimed I could uncramp them if I concentrated properly. I concentrated. I ordered my legs to uncramp. It wasn't working.

The last time my legs cramped, I had leaped up without a thought and stamped my feet. Maman had been furious. "What if someone was in the house, you stupid girl!" Maman had never spoken to me like that before. Marc said, "Maman, it was an accident. She didn't mean to—"

"No," Maman said. "No excuses. Everything each of us does now matters. Everything. Do you understand? Karin! Answer."

"Yes," I said. "I understand."

Maman nodded. "All right, then. It won't happen again." Her eyes had that swollen look, as if she'd been crying for hours.

I bit that place below my thumb where it was still a little fleshy. My skin tasted salty. When the war ended, I planned to eat everything I wanted to, salty and sweet, and no turnips or cabbage ever again. Madame Zetain was very fond of turnip stew and cabbage soup, and turnip and cabbage stew, and cabbage and turnip soup. Whatever it was, I ate it all—and whatever it was, it was never enough.

I breathed in, breathed out, deep slow breaths from my belly, the way Maman had taught me. I breathed and listened. Listened with ears, eyes, skin. Listened for a door slamming. For heavy footsteps and voices shouting, *Come out, Jews, we know you're in there.*

2

HER BEAUTIFUL EYES

"KARIN, YOU'VE mastered the art of quiet," Maman said. She sat on the mattress next to me, brushing and braiding my hair.

The art of quiet. What words! Elegant, like Maman. Of course, we were *all* quiet as mice. But every day, I still had to remind myself. I missed noise. Sometimes in my dreams I heard banging crashes, shouts, even a whole brass band.

"Maman." I whispered, as usual. "If I were to draw those words—"

"What words?"

"Maman! 'The art of quiet.' I'd draw me wrapped from chin to toes in a sort of dark blankety thing, with swirls of gray stuff, like clouds, all around."

"Lovely," she said, and started on the second braid, pulling the strands tight. Every day, Maman braided my hair. If the soldiers came, I would be taken away with my hair in smooth, tight braids.

Maman tied a piece of string around the braid. "There," she said. "Done."

I moved closer to her and thought about crawling into her lap. But I was too old for that. I had to be mature. Because of hiding, because of the war, because, as Maman said, our lives had changed and anything could happen, anytime, to any of us. Even to her.

I slid as close as I could get. I breathed in the smell of Maman, closed my eyes, and told myself another story, my favorite story of all.

I'm walking down a long sandy road. There are tall trees on both sides, the sky is big and blue like the sea, and behind me are Maman, Papa, Marc, and Grand-mère. We're together again. They're all here, my be-loveds, watching as I dance down the road under the blue, blue sky.

"Maman," I said, just to say her name.

"Yes, darling?" She looked at me.

Her smile, into which I fell with love.

Her eyes, her beautiful, beautiful eyes. Her beautiful, sad eyes.

Here was what I'd learned about sadness—it was catching. Get in the way of someone else's sadness, and before you knew it, you had it, too. And then time collapsed, and turned the day so shapeless you couldn't see to the end of it.

That's when I learned something else—to turn away from Maman's eyes. Away from the sadness. Away from thoughts of Papa and Grand-mère, of home and our little cat, Minot, and of friends and school. Yes, just turn away.

But then there was the other thing I learned—that sometimes I couldn't do it. I *had* to look at Maman. I couldn't live without looking at her.

So I did. I looked at her. And I never stopped looking. And loving her. Loving her so much.

3

No Windows

THIS ROOM where we lived was once a closet. A storage closet under the eaves, with two shelves, a black trunk, eight metal hooks, and a single lightbulb hanging from the ceiling. It measured seven of Marc's feet one way, four the other.

In this room, nearly a year had passed. I had grown taller, thinner, quieter.

Was a year a long time, or a short time? Long, surely. Yet sometimes it seemed that time itself had

been swallowed up, and that we had never lived anywhere but here, or in any other way.

Sometimes everything that was once real seemed
unreal, as if only this room was real. Marc called it
the Box. It *was* small. "Not small," he said. "Tiny,
crammed, crowded." We lived in it like mice in a nest.
"You mean rats in a hole," he said.

On the very first night we came here, I was ready to
love Madame Zetain, because she took us into her
house to hide and also—maybe mostly—because her
eyes were almost the same tiny emerald shape as
Grand-mère's. But soon I saw that Madame Zetain's
eyes slid over me, while Grand-mère could never get
enough of looking at me and talking to me. Madame
only said things like yes and no and "You stay in the
room, you."

Since I couldn't love Madame, I wanted to like her.
It would have been easier, though, if she didn't fold her
hands over her belly when she came to collect the rent
from Maman. And if she was politer to Maman. And if
we didn't all have to try so hard to make her smile.

Maman said it was sinful to go on about Madame's
manners and forget the risk she was taking, forget that
she was doing a brave thing. The German soldiers
could come anytime, sweeping into the village in their
trucks, with their dogs and guns. *Jew hunt*, they called
it. And if they found us, then Madame would be taken,

too. *Jew lover*, they would call her. That was almost as big a crime as being a Jew.

Madame said that if the soldiers came, she'd rush up the attic stairs and shove the big wooden wardrobe in front of our door. But what if she couldn't get up here ahead of them? What if they heard something? Smelled something? What if they pushed the wardrobe aside?

But it was best not to think of that.

Think, instead, of the roof. It leaked. Madame had given us two old pots for when it rained. I liked to gaze at the stains on the ceiling. They resembled brown clouds, or mushrooms like the morels that Grand-mère picked in the spring in the woods outside Paris.

The finest thing about the room was the window in the far wall, a big, clear pane of glass, through which I could see the sky—clouds, sun, stars, and moon. I could see them all, day or night, any time I wished, since the window existed only in my mind.

Sometimes I dreamed about real windows, the ones in our apartment at 86 rue Erlanger. Narrow windows, tall as doors. Windows that opened out to let in voices and the honking, hooting sounds of the city and fresh, cool air.

Sometimes I heard the sounds of schoolchildren on the street outside Madame Zetain's house. One day, I was sure I heard a girl calling, "Odette! Walk with me."

14

"Marc," I whispered, "what if it's Odette Marie Breton?" Marc raised his eyebrows, as if my question wasn't worth answering.

He was right. Odette Marie was safely home at 80 rue Erlanger with her family. She and I used to walk to school together. Did she know that I was gone? Gone from our school like all the Jewish girls—yes, of course she knew that. But gone from the street, from the city? Where did she think I went? Maybe she thought the same thing happened to me as to Sarah Olinski. Taken in a roundup by the Germans. Or maybe she didn't think about it at all.

If I wasn't who I was and where I was, would I want to think about such things?

When I asked Marc this question, he said, "You're now out of the realm of reality and, therefore, there's no possible answer."

4

THE POSTCARD

EVERY MORNING, I was the first one awake. First on my feet, first dressed, first out of the room. Maman slept in, and Marc, the minute he woke, began reading. I couldn't understand it. This was the best chance, sometimes the only chance in a day, to leave the Box. We could go downstairs to wash and use the bathroom without hurrying. Madame was not so nervous about visitors this early in the morning.

I ran barefoot across the attic floor and down the steps. At the bottom, I turned and ran back up lightly and silently. I did it again. Down and up. I thrilled myself with my light dancing feet. Down again, and up, and down.

I was panting, my face was warm. I drew in a breath, then opened the door to the kitchen. A jar of wildflowers was on the table. A wonderful smell filled the air. Biscuits? Madame Zetain was sitting at the table.

"Good morning, madame."

"Yes," she said, and covered her food with her hand, as if I might steal it. I would have liked to do that! I imagined leaping across the kitchen, snatching a biscuit, then stuffing it into my mouth.

"Barefoot again?" Madame said. "What a little savage you are. That's not how nice French girls acted when I was growing up."

"Yes, madame."

"Tell your mother it's the end of the month."

"Yes, madame."

"Tell your mother I have sewing for her."

"Yes, madame. Would you have work for me, also?"

"Certainly not."

Marc sometimes scrubbed the floors for Madame, and Maman sewed, which meant they got to leave the Box. "I'm sure I'm a good worker, madame."

She waved her hand. *"Phfft,"* she said. "Go ahead, go wash."

In the bathroom, with its damp smell, I splashed

water over my face. I stared at myself in the mirror. My face was pale, my chin was pointy. My eyes were too deep. Marc was handsome, as well as brilliant and kind. God got lazy when it was my turn. "*Phfft,*" I said, waving my hand at myself. Madame was right. I was a savage, worrying about silly things like being pretty.

Maman was awake when I went back. "Did you say good morning politely to Madame?" she asked.

"Yes, Maman. Yes yes yes yes." Maman asked the same question every morning. "She has sewing for you. She says it's the end of the month."

Maman nodded. "Brush your hair. I'll go down now."

I slung myself on the mattress, untied my braids, and brushed a few strokes. "Why does it matter if I brush my hair? Marc. Marc! Did you hear me?"

He was lying on his back, on the floor, with a book held above his head. "What?"

"No one sees me, except you and Maman. What if I didn't brush? What if my hair was tangled all day, what then?"

"You know what Maman says, Karin."

"I know, Marc! Maman says we have to carry on as normally as possible."

Normal meant that every day we had what Maman called a routine. We brushed, we washed, we exercised and studied. We kept our space neat, we weren't rude, and we never complained.

"We're not normal," I said. "How can we be normal?"

Marc turned a page. "I don't see horns growing out of your head."

"Marc. We are not living normal life. No normal life. Nothing normal anymore. No no no no. No normal life."

"Go on, brush," Marc said. He never lifted his eyes from the page.

The night we left home, we had stuffed sweaters and underwear into our knapsacks. At the last moment, I had taken paper for drawing and Marc had taken books.

"Marc, will you be a language teacher like Maman someday? If you take after Maman, then I should take after Papa. Which means I'll be a journalist instead of an artist when I grow up."

"Mmm," he said. "If you grow up."

"What? What did you say?"

"Nothing. Forget it."

If I grow up. I heard him. *If.* I tugged the brush through my hair. I brushed and counted. Every night before going to sleep, Grand-mère had brushed her hair one hundred strokes, and then we would talk.

"Marc, do you ever think about Grand-mère and Papa?"

"You know the answer."

"What?" I said.

"Stop!" he ordered.

"I suppose you do think about them. I do, but I don't like to. I feel too horrible."

"I know," Marc said. He checked his watch. It had been Papa's. This, plus the postcard, was all we had now of Papa. I knew the postcard by heart.

My dear family...I write this to you from a room in this place. Drancy. I am here with many other people, all of us waiting. We have been waiting for hours. It is hell here. I will say no more about it. My only consolation is that you have been spared this. Soon we'll be on a train going to Poland. They tell us that we will be put to work there. If so, many of us would welcome it. But there are children here—many little ones, many without their parents—and they are also going on the train. Will they work, too? I have a plan, so don't worry about me. I love you all more than life itself. Remember me. Your devoted husband and father, Aleksander Levi

"Marc."

"Yes, what now?"

"Do you think Aunt Hannah Greenwald would invite us to visit her in America?"

"She might."

"Would you like to go there?"

"Of course."

"But only with Maman," I said.

Aunt Hannah was Papa's mother's sister, so she was really Great-aunt Hannah. We had never met her, as she had lived in America since she was fifteen.

"Marc, remember Alena?"

"Who, now?"

"Alena. She was the one who told us we had to leave home, because the Germans were planning another roundup. And they knew about us, because of Papa's trying to escape from the train and being shot." I stopped. It was hard to breathe. "Marc, you remember Alena, don't you? Don't you?" I said, as if it mattered. "She drove us here."

"Oh, her. Yes."

"She was so tall, and she smoked, one cigarette after another." She had been a colleague of Papa's at the newspaper. She was the one who brought us the postcard. She was the one who found Madame Zetain for us.

"Brush, Karin," Maman said.

When had she come back? "Yes, Maman. I'm almost done. Did you sew already for Madame?"

"No, I'll go down later. Marc, go wash."

"At once," Marc said. He didn't move.

That morning, we each had an egg. Fantastic! "Madame's visitor brought her a basket of fresh eggs," Maman said.

We ate, sitting around the trunk. It was our table, our couch, our desk, and sometimes Marc's bed, although usually he slept on a heap of Monsieur Zetain's old clothes. Softer, but smelly. Monsieur Zetain had died six years before. I couldn't decide which was worse, the old-clothes smell or the mouse-pee smell on the mattress that Maman and I shared.

When it was time for lessons, Maman gave an assignment to write a true story. "Make it a happy one, yes?" Marc had to write his story in French and English. I didn't feel like writing in any language.

"I'll draw my story," I said.

"We're writing today," Maman whispered in her teacher voice. She bent close. I breathed in her smell and reached for her hand. "Maman, I love you."

"And I love you," she said. "Now write your story."

"And it has to be happy?"

"Surely you have one happy story to tell. I know you do."

A True Story
by Karin Levi

I always loved birthdays, especially mine. I loved waking up and being one year older, and I loved getting presents and having a cake and hearing everyone sing "Happy Birthday." Two years ago, on the night before my eighth birthday, which was Thursday night, June 13, 1940, I was watching Grand-mère brush her hair and I was feeling scared because of the Germans bombing our city and, at the same time, I was thinking about a lot of things, not all of them so serious.

I was thinking about presents and birthday cake. And I was thinking that tomorrow, when I was eight, I would feel more grown-up and be a more serious person. But right then I was still the same. And I still loved presents, and I hadn't seen any hidden around the house.

I knew I wasn't going to have a birthday cake, because all the pastry shops were closed. None of the stores and shops was open, because of the bombing and all the people leaving the city. We heard the bombs, and it was so scary. But we were lucky, because none of them had dropped near us.

Our neighbors across the hall and above us and right below us were gone. They were the Beaulois, the Camus, and the Chabrons, and they had all left.

Maman, you wanted to go, too, but Papa said we would stay, he had a job to do for the newspaper. And when we heard on the radio that German planes had strafed people on the highway and hundreds and hundreds of people had died, we knew he had been right.

Papa told us that every road out of Paris was jammed with cars, bicycles, wagons, wheelbarrows, baby carriages, and even go-carts. And even though the bombs scared me, and even though the Germans were coming closer, I was glad we were in our own home.

I was thinking about all of that on the night before my birthday. But I didn't actually like to think about it. And as I was still only seven then, I thought about cake instead. Two or three times I said to Grand-mère, "I *love* chocolate cake."

"I know you do, darling," she said each time, and she kept on brushing her hair very slowly, as if she was extra tired.

She made her nightgown like a tent and got undressed underneath it. She got into bed next to me, gave me my kiss, and we went to sleep. In the morning, when I woke up, I kissed her cheek, and said, "Good morning, Grand-mère." Usually, she would wake right up with me. I got out of bed and went to look out the window. The street was empty and quiet. I kept waiting for Grand-mère to wake up. I said, "Grand-mère, time to get up." I kissed her again. "Grand-mère." I called her name louder, but she never moved.

When the doctor came, he said her heart

had stopped while she was sleeping. "A painless death," he said, and he tied her jaws together with a white cloth.

The next thing I remember is standing at the window, and Marc was by me, and we were watching German soldiers march down our street. "Good for Grand-mère," Marc said. "She had the sense to die before she had to see the rotten Germans here."

I thought he meant it was good that Grand-mère had died, and I hated him.

No one remembered my birthday. I didn't care. I remember thinking that next year my birthday would have to be better. But by then, more bad things had happened, so it wasn't.

I'm sorry, Maman, not to write a happy story. I'll try again.

My Best Friend
by Karin Levi

My best friend in school was Sarah Olinski. We both loved to roller-skate, read, and draw, although Sarah loved to read more than I did, and I loved to draw more than she did. Also, I was noisy and talkative and she was shy. Otherwise, we were very well matched.

I loved her curly red hair. She said she liked my dark straight hair better. We each had an older brother and a grandmother who lived with us. "So, except for our hair, we're as alike as twins," we would say.

Once I went with Sarah to her home near Père Lachaise cemetery. It was in the same arrondissement where Papa had a room when he had come to Paris as a student and was poor. I never thought about what *poor* meant until I saw where Sarah lived. The streets were crumbly and dirty, and so narrow that every time a car or horse and wagon came through, we had to press up against a building so they wouldn't run us down.

Sarah's family lived on the fourth floor, but they had no elevator. Their three rooms weren't even as big as our living room. Her papa worked on his sewing machine in the kitchen, and they used a Turkish toilet down the hall, which is a hole in the floor where you squat and do your business.

We went up to the roof to get privacy and talk about our plans. Our main plan was to be best friends forever until we were old, old ladies. But first we would go on to lycée together. "We *hope*," Sarah always said, because she would have to take the scholarship exam and everybody knew not many passed. "But you will," I said. "And after lycée, we'll go to university together." The rest of our plan was for her to be a famous writer and me to be a famous artist. We also planned to each get married and have two children, boy and girl, who would all be friends.

After the Germans came, we didn't talk much about plans. Every day, it seemed, the Germans made another rule for us. No bikes for Jews. No phones for Jews. No pets for Jews. We joked that Sarah was lucky her family couldn't afford bikes and phones, so she didn't have to miss them, like I did. And when they took our radios away, we joked that they were putting Jewish radios in jail.

Then they didn't allow us to go to parks or on the trains. After that, no movies and no library. My family had to give up Minot, even though she had been with us since she was a tiny kitty. Some people said the Germans were killing Jews' pets, but others said our pets were given away to nice families. Sarah and I pretended we knew Minot was happy with a new family.

Then we all had to wear the yellow star of David on our clothes. The first day Sarah and I appeared at school with the stars, some girls called us Yids and pushed us around in the school yard. Sylvie Menard, who had always been friendly before, came up smiling and said, "Karin! Did you see the sign on the police station? 'No Jews, Negroes, or Dogs Allowed.' That's what they should put up on our school."

One of the big girls, Monique, pushed Sarah and spit at her. I spit back, and Monique screamed as if I'd tried to kill her. "Go to Palestine, Jew-girl!" she yelled.

"Where's that?" I said.

It was all horrible, and I think Sarah, who never said a word, suffered the most. Not too long after that, she and all her family were taken away in a roundup, and we never heard anything about them again.

Maman, I'm sorry I wandered off the happy part of the story.

5

RENT MONEY

"MADAME, COME IN, please. What a pleasure," Maman said, as if she were in our own home on rue Erlanger.

Madame Zetain stepped into the attic room.

At a glance from Maman, Marc jumped up from the trunk, banging his head on the rafter. "Please, madame, sit down."

"Not necessary."

We all stood in silence, stooped over because of the low ceiling.

"The lentil soup this morning was so good, madame," I said. "It was delicious, the best I ever ate. I could have eaten much more." I hoped that didn't sound as if she hadn't given us enough. She hadn't, of course, but to say so would be rude.

Madame Zetain folded her hands over her belly. "You have to leave," she said.

Maman stood there, the rent money in her outstretched hand.

"You don't mean leave *here*, madame?" Marc said. He sat down.

My eyes flew around the room. The trunk, the shelves, the mattress, Marc's books, the heap of old clothes that was his bed.

How could we leave? This was where we lived now.

"People are talking," Madame Zetain said. "This is a small town, and they talk. I'm sorry. I never knew you would be here so long."

"But, madame, where will we go?" Maman spoke at last.

"They're saying things, saying that I'm hiding... hiding Jews." She was stuttering. "They've heard things—noises."

"No," Maman said. "No. You know how quiet we are."

Madame Zetain's eye twitched. "You have to go, all of you. Tonight."

6

BOILED POTATOES

IN THE FARMYARD, a rooster crowed. A dog barked without stopping. Maman sucked in her breath. Lately she had become afraid of dogs. "He's tied up, Maman," I said. I bent over and held out a hand. "Hello, boy. Hello, good boy."

The dog barked and barked, his lips drawn back in a frothy snarl. I went around him to the door and knocked.

Maman sat on a rock, well away from the dog, and rubbed her swollen feet. She had been hobbling in her elegant Parisian shoes, until the heels broke off. She had always worn beautiful, soft leather shoes with slender heels. Now the heels were gone and the shoes were like slippers.

The farmhouse door opened slowly. "What?" a voice said.

"Good morning," Maman said. Sudden energy in her voice. She stood up. "May I speak to you for a moment, madame?"

The door opened wider. A woman in a plain blue dress and a man's gray cardigan stood there. "Hello," I said. Behind her, I saw a table set with bowls and mugs. An iron pot on a stove. A cot in a corner. It had been weeks since I'd slept on a real bed, in a real room.

"Would you have a place for me and my children to rest for a few hours today?" Maman held herself straight in the muddy yard.

"I have nothing." The door began to close.

A man appeared from around the side of the house. "What do they want, Edith?" He was dressed in overalls and muddy rubber boots.

"We need to rest, monsieur," Maman said. "We've been walking—"

"Henri, tell them we have nothing for them," the woman said. "Barely enough for ourselves. It's these times—"

"Our house was bombed," I said quickly. This was

the story we'd agreed to. "We lost everything. We're lucky we got out with our lives."

"Ahhh," the woman said.

I couldn't tell whether she believed me or not. "We're going to my aunt Madelein in Aix-les-Bains. She'll let us stay with her, even though she's very poor herself. I'll sleep with my cousins Anne and Lara in their room." As I said this, I saw it all as if it existed. My aunt in the little apartment, my girl cousins sleeping in the room off the kitchen.

Maman swayed. Marc caught her by the arm. "My mother's very tired." He spoke quietly, but I saw the blaze of anger race up his cheeks.

Ever since we'd left Madame Zetain's house, we had walked at night and slept during the day wherever we could—in the woods, a deserted house, sometimes in a farmer's barn with other people like ourselves. At night, the roads were empty and safer. If a car was coming, we'd be warned by the light fanning into the air, and we'd run into the fields or slide into a ditch until the car was gone.

We were walking south. The Italians were there in the south of France, and even though they were the Germans' allies, they didn't hate Jews. At least, that's what people said. Besides, Maman had an old friend, Paulette Ophels, who lived in a town called Valence, right near the border. Maman and Paulette had attended the Sorbonne together years before. Maman said they'd been out of touch, but she was sure Paulette would help us.

"Can we stay, or not?" Marc said to the farmwoman.

"Excuse my son's rudeness," Maman said. "We're all so tired." Maman knew how to talk to people. Gentle, quiet.

"They can sleep in the barn," the man said to the woman.

"Can you give us food?" Marc asked. "We have a little bit of money, and I can work."

"We have nothing," the woman said.

"Get them something to eat, Edith," the man said. "For god's sake, woman." He stamped into the house. She followed and closed the door. Slammed it.

We stood in the yard. Rain spattered on my face. The dog barked. A crow flew over, calling in his hoarse voice. Lucky crow. Wings to take him home.

The man came out and handed Maman a chunk of bread, then led us behind the house to a barn. He kicked his muddy boots against the wall and pointed to the hayloft above the cow's stall. "The hay's clean," he said, then went away.

We climbed into the loft and mounded up the hay for beds. Maman took off her shoes and rubbed her feet. Rain fell steadily against the roof.

The man came back and handed up a pail of milk.

"You could leave the boy here," he said. "Are you a good worker?" he asked Marc. "I can use another pair of hands. You'll be safe with me."

"Leave my son?" Maman said. "Oh, I don't—"

"Let the boy speak for himself. How old are you, boy, thirteen?"

"No, monsieur. Twelve." Marc's neck had turned red.

"Old enough to work," the man said.

Marc kicked the wall, as the man had. "Monsieur, my mother and my sister, I have to, you know, I have to take care of them!"

The man shrugged.

"Thank you for the milk, monsieur," Maman said.

"What's bread without milk," he said flatly, and left.

"Monsieur," I called after him. I had just tasted the milk. "This is the best milk I ever had!"

Later, when it was dark, we knocked on the door to thank the farmer and his wife. The woman handed Maman a little sack of boiled potatoes. "The Germans," she said, "they've brought us all nothing but evil, isn't that so?" She refused to take money.

7

WALKING SOUTH

AND SO WE continued walking south, avoiding daylight and people and towns. We walked through dry, moonless black nights and nights when rain fell steadily. Some nights the wind gusted and blew us down the road, and one night a perfectly full white moon lit the road in front of us like a torch.

We saw signs of the war everywhere. Stumps where trees had been. Burned fields, broken houses. We came across abandoned military trucks and even some tanks tipped over on their sides.

I was startled by our freedom, startled and frightened by how alone we were, the way we passed down these strange roads, reeling through an almost empty world.

Sometimes, even with my eyes open, I knew I was sleeping, and the world seemed to tremble and shake in the darkness. I staggered after Maman and Marc. To walk and yet sleep became almost ordinary. To walk at night and sleep in the day did become ordinary. It was one more bit of the world turned upside down and inside out.

So much came to me like that now—in doubles and in opposites, as yes and no, as one thing and then another.

We were free and unfree.

We were in our own beloved land, but it was not ours.

We moved loosely, even boldly, our feet eating the miles, but in a single moment we could lose everything, freedom and one another.

We wanted the darkness, but we feared it. Dogs barked in the night. Roads were unfamiliar. And to be discovered in the night would shout out who we were— Jews, running away.

Asleep on the floor of an abandoned shack, an arm over my eyes, or curled on the ground in a weedy field, I dreamed of dark streets and of the beach near the ocean. I dreamed of flying, of leaping through the sky.

I dreamed of Papa and my cat and cookies. And always I dreamed about food. I was hungry all the time. In my dreams, I ate huge meals, but when I woke up, I was still hungry.

It was always the same when I was awake. Wanting food. Looking for it. Food and water. Water—a pond, a puddle, a brook—any water. And when we found it, we would drink and wash, sit beside it, and be happy in the little moment. And then we would walk again.

8

THE OLD MAN

WE REACHED Valence at last. We were hungry and not very clean. I was stunned to be among buildings and people again, and frightened at how exposed we were, how everyone could see us.

At the address where Maman had hoped to find her friend, the man who opened the door said, "Who?"

"Paulette Ophels," Maman repeated, her hand to her chest. She was breathing hard from the climb up three flights of stairs.

"Never heard of her." He looked us over carefully. "What did you say your name was?"

Maman had not said.

My chest was suddenly tight. The man had recognized us as Jews. "Maman." I tugged her hand. "Let's go." I bolted down the stairs.

Outside, we walked quickly away. In a square filled with people selling things, we stopped at a fountain and drank and washed our faces. A group of soldiers came toward us. "Maman," I said.

"Italian," Maman murmured. "Not German."

The outdoor market filled the square and spilled into the side streets. People were crowded together, their wares laid out on wagons and tables, on boxes and on blankets spread out on the ground.

Marc found us a space between a woman selling meat pies and another selling a pair of children's shoes. On a sheet of newspaper, we laid out an embroidered handkerchief, a tortoiseshell hair clip that had been Grand-mère's, and a little leather purse. We had nothing else of value except Papa's watch, which Marc kept on a loop on his belt.

We waited for customers. People passed and glanced at our things, but no one stopped. Maman sat on the ground. Marc wandered off.

I stayed standing. The meat pies nearby smelled so good. I remembered stories I'd read about starving people boiling shoes to make soup. Maybe we'd have to boil the little purse. Make leather soup.

An old man stopped. He was dressed in black: a

black suit, black hat, black shoes. "A fine handkerchief," he said, squinting.

"Hand embroidered, monsieur," I said. The linen square had a flower in one corner and tiny leaves worked around the edges. "My maman did it."

"Embroidery is an art," the old man said.

"I agree, monsieur," Maman said.

"Excellent work, madame. I congratulate you. Yes, yes, excellent!"

Buy it, I wished at him. As soon as he paid Maman, I would buy a meat pie and break it into three parts. Or maybe it would be better to buy three eggs. A man farther down the aisle was selling peeled hard-boiled eggs from a jar.

The old man told Maman about a trip he'd taken to Paris when he was twenty-one, or was it twenty-two? No, no, twenty-one; he was a boy then, and so naive, madame! "And you and your children come from Paris, too, madame," he said. "I can hear it in your voice! I know accents. I do. I do."

If only he would stop talking and take out his purse. "The handkerchief. Would you like to buy it, monsieur?" I asked. I almost added, *Yes or no?* but caught Maman's glance.

"I'm considering buying it. Yes, yes, I am." But on he went, talking about Paris and staring first into Maman's face, then mine.

I looked away. There was something strange about this old man. He was stoop shouldered, with a tangled salt-and-pepper beard. Why would he be so interested in an embroidered handkerchief? Maybe he was a police spy. People like that were all around, like dogs, sniffing out Jews.

I saw Marc walking back, weaving through the crowds with a loaf of bread under his arm. As soon as he saw us, he began tearing off chunks. He gave a chunk to me and another to Maman. I stuffed the bread in my mouth. "Where'd you get it?" I asked him.

"Never mind."

The old man had been talking to Maman. Now he bent over and helped her up. "My name is Jean Taubert, madame," he said in a low voice. I had to strain to hear him. "I am officially stupid. Harmless."

Marc and I glanced at each other. *Officially stupid?*

"I have an offer." The old man picked up the handkerchief and examined it again. "Shelter." He said this word so softly I wasn't sure if I had really heard him.

Maman stuffed our things into the knapsack. The old man took it from her, and they walked off.

I stood there, staring. It didn't seem real, Maman walking away with a stranger, leaving us.

"What's she doing?" Marc said. "Who is that man?"

I grabbed his hand, and we broke into a run.

9

A TALL, NARROW HOUSE

MONSIEUR TAUBERT lived in a tall, narrow house in a cobblestoned alleyway. It was a dark, old man's house, with lumpy furniture and stacks of newspapers in the corners. Three other people lived there, Jews like ourselves. Redheaded Simone, her uncle Leo, and Bernard, a little boy. They looked us over coldly.

Monsieur Taubert said we were hungry. Simone brought a pot from the stove and set it down on the table. She put out three spoons, three bowls. The soup was good. There was bread, too. I asked for a second bowl of soup and got it. Then suddenly, I wanted to sleep more than anything in the world.

For the first time in weeks, I was inside, in a house, in a room, safe. And there was a bed against the wall. I lay down. I heard Maman say something. I heard Simone answer, "No, Uncle Leo and I are from—" And then I fell asleep.

Later I found out they were from Rouen. Simone and her uncle Leo were all that remained of their family. They had escaped a transport. The boy, Bernard, had lost his parents and sisters, and found Simone and attached himself to her. He was a funny little boy. He hardly said anything. When he did speak, his voice was high and squeaky.

Monsieur Taubert had taken them all in off the street.

"He's a saint," Simone said.

Maman agreed. "A genuine human being."

I was suspicious and uneasy, but they were right. Just as Maman said, Monsieur Taubert was a good man. It was as simple as that.

Maman tried to keep us to our routine, but she wasn't well. Almost from the day we began living in Monsieur's house, she grew weak. It was as if she had held herself together until we were safe and then let go.

When she could, she taught us—including Bernard—our lessons. Sometimes Marc was there, sometimes not. He had begun to leave the house, to go off on his own. He wouldn't say where. "Here and there" was the way he put it. "Only God knows" was the way Maman put it.

Marc said he looked for work around the market, carrying bundles or unloading wagons. Sometimes he brought back money or food. Once he brought us three oranges, which we divided among us all. We each had almost half an orange. They were marvelous. We couldn't stop talking about them.

Marc's voice was changing. Before he went out, he would say in his new deep voice, "Maman, be easy. I'm careful." As if saying that would stop her from worrying. He knew better, but it wasn't only his voice that was changing: He'd become a little bit selfish. He did what he wanted. He was often gone for hours.

"Let me go with him, Maman," I said. I wanted to go out, too. When I thought of the weeks we'd traveled, I forgot about being hungry and scared and only remembered how free I'd been. "I'll stay with him, Maman," I said. "I'll watch him and keep him safe."

"No," Maman said. "I wouldn't have a moment's peace. You think you're missing something, darling?" A coughing spasm shook her. It was the damp in the house, she said, that made her cough and feel tired all the time.

"You think it's safe out there?" she said. "It's not."

She was right about that, too.

Monsieur had two radios. One was large, prominently placed in the living room. The other, a shortwave in a small mahogany box, was hidden in the cellar. At night, Monsieur brought it out and we listened to the BBC from London for news of the war. That was how we heard that Italy had surrendered.

At first, we rejoiced. Italy had been Germany's main ally. We thought this meant the end of the war. But it meant instead that the Italian soldiers left Valence and the Germans moved in. Within days, they began conducting house-to-house searches for Jews.

10

GOOD-BYE FOR NOW

THE FLOOR under the coal bin in the cellar was dirt. We moved the coal aside and dug a pit where we could hide if the Germans came. We practiced lying in that tiny space. Monsieur Taubert covered us with boards, then moved the coal back. We lay there, packed together in silence, as if the Germans were in the house. An hour later, when he let us out, Maman fainted.

We had already hidden away anything—bedding, books, clothes—that would reveal our presence. But even that wasn't enough. Valence had become too dangerous. We had to leave—leave Monsieur, leave Valence, leave France—and cross the mountains into Italy. Monsieur knew people who would help us.

Late one night, he woke us and told us to get ready. Marc and I were the first ones downstairs. Then the others—Simone, Uncle Leo, and Bernard. "Shall we go?" Bernard said in his high voice.

"Karin and Marc's maman isn't here yet." Uncle Leo put his hands on Bernard's shoulders. "We'll leave together, all at the same time. That's the way, isn't it?"

We stood around, our knapsacks at our feet, waiting for Maman. Bernard leaned against Uncle Leo. Simone paced. The room was dark, with only a little light filtering in from outside.

"Where is she?" Simone said.

"She'll come," Uncle Leo said. He was always calm.

Marc went to the stairwell. "Maman?"

At last, we heard her coming slowly down the stairs. "Sorry, everyone." She was panting. "I'm...ready." She leaned, slumped really, against the wall.

"This is absurd," Simone said. "She's sick, she's too weak." She picked up her knapsack. "How will she do this? She'll never make it two steps."

I glared at Simone. "We'll help her!"

Maman took my arm. "Shhh." Her face was shiny with sweat.

"We still have a moment," Monsieur Taubert said. "Rest yourself," he urged Maman. "Sit down."

She started to protest, but then she sat down on the couch and put her head back. Her eyes closed. We waited. Five minutes passed. Ten minutes.

"Well...," Monsieur said.

"We have to go," Simone said. "Now."

Monsieur bent over Maman and spoke quietly. "Why not stay here? Let the children leave tonight. When you're stronger, you'll follow."

"I won't go without my mother," I said. I sat down next to her.

"If Maman stays, we will, too," Marc said.

And that was it. We hugged and kissed the others, wished them a safe journey, and watched them leave without us.

In the weeks that followed, Maman had some good days, but most of the time she lay on the couch, wrapped in a blanket. She slept a lot, and we were glad. Monsieur said rest was the best cure.

One afternoon, we heard that German soldiers were in the neighborhood. We woke Maman and helped her downstairs to the cellar, to the hole under the coal bin. It was torture for her to lie there. The soldiers never came, but by the time Monsieur let us out, Maman had fainted again.

The weather turned cooler and rain came. We had a second scare. A German soldier came to the door, and we had no time to go to the cellar. The soldier entered the house as we hid in the broom closet. We could hear everything.

"What a job," Monsieur said, "rounding up Jews, that lot of filth. One good thing, the Italian scum are gone." He offered the soldier a drink. The soldier said something in German, and Monsieur Taubert laughed. "I've a little bit saved," he said, "for the right occasion."

In the closet, we held ourselves still. Marc's arm was twisted behind his back. Maman's body shook, but she never let out a sound.

The start of the new year came and passed. The Germans were everywhere, arresting people off the street. Marc had stopped going out. Monsieur, in order to avoid attracting attention, was more careful than ever about what he brought into the house. There wasn't much food.

Maman wanted Marc and me to leave, but we argued with her. "No, Maman. We're not going without you. We won't!"

"I hope," she said one day, sitting up on the couch and holding the blanket close around her, "that I still

have something to say about what my children do!"
She sounded like her old self for a moment. "I hope
that I haven't lost every shred of authority."

"No, Maman, of course not," we said, but we kept
delaying. Marc got a cold. I got a sore throat. The soles
of his shoes were worn through, and he had to fix them.
One thing after another.

There were fewer and fewer excuses. But not until
Monsieur Taubert told us that he was getting Maman
false identification papers—Maman would live there as
his widowed sister—did we agree to go.

On the night we left, Maman held me. "Don't be
sad, darling. As soon as I'm stronger, I'll follow you."

"And you'll find us," I said.

"I will. I promise. Now say good-bye to me."

I was crying.

"It's only for now," Maman said.

I kissed her hand and then her face, kissed it again
and again.

A small truck waited on a tree-lined street. Two men
sat in front, smoking. We went up to them. "Good
evening," I said. "Do you know my uncle Henri?"

One of the men flicked ash out the window. "Know
him well."

That was the signal.

We went around to the back of the truck. Marc climbed up and reached down to help me. The heavy canvas flap fell down behind us.

Darkness.

"Marc," I whispered.

"Quiet," a woman's voice ordered.

The truck jerked into motion, and I was thrown back against a bench. I sat down abruptly, sensing people on both sides. Marc squeezed in next to me. I heard sounds of breathing. A muffled sneeze.

The truck jolted along. The engine labored as we climbed higher. The hours passed, and I dozed. Once I dreamed that Maman and I were sitting on the blue couch at home, looking at a photo album. "Here's Papa and me on vacation," Maman said. I strained to see Papa's face. A breeze blew white curtains over the album.... Marc was shaking my arm, pulling me up. Everyone was getting off the truck.

Outside, it was dark and chilly, with a glimmer of moonlight in the sky. All around us were mountains. The air was cold and damp, and I huddled inside my sweater. "Where are we?" I asked.

Marc pointed. "Italy, that way," he said.

11

TO THE HILLS

WE WERE walking again by night and sleeping where we could during the day. The Germans were everywhere on the main roads and in the railroad stations. We were going south again. The south of Italy, where the Americans were, where we would be safe, where we could wait for Maman to join us. We stayed high in the hills above the sea. All we had to do was keep the sea on our right and the morning sun on our left.

Often, I was half asleep as we walked, holding on to Marc's sleeve, the way I had when it was he and

Maman and I. But then we had been in France. Now France was far behind us. And so was Maman.

Sometimes, at night, we found ourselves walking alongside other refugees, people without homes, looking for a safe place.

At a farm, a young woman warned us that the Germans were nearby, in the next village. She gave us bread and cheese and pointed out a trail through the hills. That day we didn't go hungry, but the day after, we had no food at all.

Sometimes I thought of Madame Zetain's little house and of Monsieur Taubert's tall, narrow house, and they seemed like houses in a dream where, every night, I had slept in a bed under a roof and, every day, washed myself under running water and sat at a table and eaten a meal. Now our clothes were stained, our feet had become hard and callused. Marc's hair was long, mine uncombed. We looked wild, like children without a mother.

Sometimes we were so hungry, we went right into a village, boldly asking for food or work. Sometimes in a café, they'd give us stale bread or old vegetables. "*Grazie, grazie,*" I said.

I was lying under a tree, napping, when something—grunts, thuds—jolted me awake. For a moment I didn't know what I was seeing. A twist of arms and legs. Boys.

Heads ducked into a circle. A gang of boys was beating Marc with fists and feet. I screamed and ran at them. I jumped on one of them, pulled his hair, and he knocked me to the ground. A moment later, they ran off, taking our knapsack and Papa's watch.

We sat for a while, close to each other. Marc kept touching his nose to see if it was still bleeding. When it got dark, we set off again. It was still dark when we went down from the hills, moving cautiously past a sleeping village, to the sea. We washed in the cold water.

When we were done, the sun was coming up, and we saw the village clearly. We saw the houses climbing the hills, each house lavished with large windows and doors. The walls were overflowing with flowers of the most fantastic size and extraordinary color. Purples and pinks, and bright oranges and reds. It was like looking at a vast flower garden, one that had somehow been transformed into houses. Flower houses.

It took us a moment to realize that the flowers, the large windows and doors, the riotously colored walls were all painted. *Trompe l'oeil.* "Fool-the-eye painting." In fact, each little cottage had just one small door and two small windows.

12

MARIA THERESA

AFTER THOSE BOYS beat Marc and robbed us, I felt we had no one in the world who cared about us, except each other. One day the straps on my sandals broke. I cried. No, I wanted to cry, but I hadn't eaten for two days and it took too much energy to make tears.

Later that same day, a farmer gave us a ride in the back of his wagon. He fixed my sandals with twine and gave us each a sandwich. I lay back, swaying with the movement of the wagon. I saw a curving road. A horse in a field. Children playing.

Then I was showing Maman the trompe l'oeil houses with their flowered windows, and she pointed out how the artist had painted each petal of every flower in perfect detail. "This is the secret of everything," Maman said mysteriously. And I woke up, happy because my sandals were on my feet and my belly was full, and I'd just seen Maman.

One night, we slept in a church cellar, where wooden benches were stored. In the morning, a young priest gave us bread and cups of hot milk. "How are you going on this day?" he said in French that was so funny we tried not to laugh. But he laughed first. Then he offered us an old battered bicycle with broken pedals. "It goes," he said, making circling motions with his hands.

We rode away, Marc peddling and me sitting behind him, on the fender. It was a bumpy ride, but the countryside sped by. Then, going down a hill, the brakes failed. Marc dragged his feet, but the bicycle went out of control and pitched us both off. I was flying and then I was in a ditch.

Marc lay on the ground, his eyes shut. I staggered to my feet and called his name. "Open your eyes," I ordered. "Marc!" He was scaring me.

A tall, almond-eyed girl straddling a bicycle watched us from the road. She was holding her hair, which was long and black and gathered into a ponytail. A bundle was strapped to the back of her bicycle. She said something to us in Italian.

Marc sat up, holding his head between his hands. The sleeve was torn off his shirt. He got up and examined our bicycle. "Look at this, Karin," he said wearily. The handlebars were twisted and the chain had come off the sprocket. "Poor old bicycle. It's dead!"

"Poor old us," I said.

The girl helped us fix the bicycle. She had big, raw-looking hands. Strong. We all set off together. Her name was Maria Theresa, and she thought the way I spoke Italian was the funniest thing she'd ever heard.

Maria Theresa liked to talk, but mainly to Marc. He knew enough Italian to make it sound like a real conversation. She told him—and he told me—about the fishing boat she'd worked on; and about the little farm her mother owned, where she was going; and about her father, Babba, who had died. She shared her food equally with us and didn't seem to care that we had nothing to give in return.

"Did you hear Maria Theresa say her mother's a healing woman?" Marc asked. We were pushing the bicycles up a steep path. It was late in the day, and Maria

Theresa was leading us higher into the hills, away from the main road. Below us, a village was already in shadows. We had heard there were Germans there.

"A wounded soldier came to their village," Marc said. "He was bleeding. Her mother wrapped his wound with a cloth she soaked in his urine and—"

"That's disgusting, Marc."

He smiled. "Pissed on the cloth, and the wound healed perfectly, Karin."

"Beautiful," I said. We walked in silence for a while. Then I said, "Marc. Do you think Maria Theresa knows we're Jews?"

"Don't twist your face like that, you look like a fish," he said. "It's either your face or your hands, all the time now. And don't worry about Maria Theresa. Like Maman always said about Monsieur Taubert, she's a good person. There are such people, you know."

I let myself fall behind. I wished he hadn't mentioned Maman. I remembered how I had said with so much confidence, *You'll find us, Maman.* How was she going to do that? Find us where? I twisted my hands together, then caught myself and tucked them under my arms.

Maria Theresa stayed with us all the rest of the way down the coast. Once, when we lay down to sleep on a hillside near some rocks, she screamed and scrambled to her feet, crossing herself. There was an arm lying on the ground. Then the wind blew toward us, and we could smell it.

We left. None of us talked about it.

Above a hillside village, where the soft rock of the cliffs was pocked with caves, Maria Theresa brought us to a small cave. "We'll rest now," she said, laying down her bicycle. "I'm home."

"Home?" I said. "This is where you live?"

"No, silly one! This is my family's cave. It's where we keep our wine and olive oil, and we hide here when danger comes. Down there is our house."

Marc and I looked where she pointed, as if we could pick out Maria Theresa's house from the others. We hunkered there, looking down the rocky slope of the mountain and listening to her. She hadn't seen her mother for six months, she said, but now she was coming with money she had earned and would stay home. "I won't leave my mama now for a long time." She was almost singing her words. She told us to sleep there by the cave, where she knew we would be safe, and she'd come back in the morning.

For a while after she left, we sat outside, looking up at the sky and listening to the wind. If only we'd had a cave like this when we had been with Maman. Our own tiny place, where nobody could find us. Where nobody could hurt us.

In the morning, Maria Theresa brought us bread, a spoon, and a pot of soup. Marc and I passed the spoon back and forth.

She had brought clothes for us, too: a skirt and a blouse for me, and a shirt of her babba's for Marc. I crawled into the cave to change. I started to daydream that we'd go with Maria Theresa to the farm, stay with her and her mother—we could work and help them— and it would be there that Maman would find us.

"Listen," she said when I came out, "I have good news. Go to Naples."

"Naples?" I said. "Why?"

"The Americans are there and they want people like you. I hear they have a big ship for you to live on. You'll be safe."

She put us on the road to Naples, and in a few days we found the Americans and the ship, which was called the *Henry Gibbins*.

It was July of 1944.

Part Two

UNITED STATES

1944 – 1945

Dearest Maman,

I'm writing to you from the middle of the Atlantic Ocean. No, I'm not in the water! (Joke, Maman.) I'm sitting on a wooden box on the deck of a troopship called the <u>Henry Gibbins</u>, on my way to America. Don't worry, Maman, Marc is with me. We boarded this ship in Naples, with a thousand other people like us. There are also a thousand wounded American soldiers on this boat, plus the crew, which makes it very crowded. President Franklin Delano Roosevelt personally sent this boat to Italy from the United States.

Marc says three thousand people wanted to get on, so it's sort of a miracle that we did. Marc told the Americans about Aunt Hannah in California and that helped. Everyone, except the Americans, is like us—no homes, hardly any clothes. I'm not the only barefoot person! My sandals fell apart in Naples, Maman, so I hop as fast as I can over the burning-hot deck.

Jo, who sleeps in the bunk below me in the women's quarters, lost her mother, her husband, and her three brothers. She comes from Sarajevo, in Yugoslavia, and she's pregnant. I like to put my hand on her belly and feel the baby move. She really wants to go to America and so does everyone else here—except me! We each had to sign a paper saying that after the war is over, we will return to our own country. A lot of people were upset, but I signed gladly.

Maman, every day the cooks throw leftover food to the gulls. They fly around the ship constantly, waiting for it. Those gulls eat better than we ever did! But now we eat two times a day, seven-thirty in the morning and five-thirty at night. Maman, American food is so strange. For breakfast, there's a cereal called cornflakes. The flakes crunch in your mouth, but if you pour milk on them, they get soft and gooey. They also have peanut butter, which you spread on bread—American bread is very soft and white. Another American food is a red, slippery, jiggly dessert called Jell-O.

Today, one of the soldiers gave me a "stick" of chewing gum. Maman, a riddle: What do you chew but never swallow? Chewing gum! But it's not really a stick. It's straight and flat and thin. Smells good. You unwrap it, put it in your mouth, and chew. Why? Because it tastes good! Like peppermint.

I said to the soldier, "Swell! Thanks, Joe GI!" He liked that. He said, "_Okay_! Only it's GI Joe, kid!" _Kid_ is an American word for a child, either a boy or a girl. Isn't it a nice American word, Maman? It's easy to say. The soldiers are especially nice to us kids. They give us sweets and teach us American words like _okay_ and _swell_ and _hubba-hubba_. One of them gave me this notebook I'm writing in. His name is Steven, and he's also Jewish. He lost a leg. He gets around on crutches with his pants leg pinned up.

There's an American lady on the ship named Ruth Gruber. She's teaching us English. She was sent by President Roosevelt, too, to help all the people. She's like a mother, because you can tell her your problems, but she looks more like a movie star! She's really beautiful, with pale skin and blond hair and red lips. Just imagine, Maman, when she came on the _Henry Gibbins_ in Naples, she climbed the rope ladder wearing white sailor pants and a white jacket. And then a sailor came after her and handed her her beautiful red pinwheel hat. We all just stared in awe.

Maman, my favorite American candy is called a Mars bar. It's delicious. Chocolate on the outside, chewy inside. I'll bring you one when I come home.

Because I _will_ come home. I never wanted to go so far away from you. I didn't want to get on this boat. But

Marc said we wouldn't be safe anywhere in Europe until the war was over, and that you would absolutely want us to do this. To go to America. To be safe. That's why I agreed, Maman. But I'm sad about it. Every moment I'm farther away from you.

Good night, darling Maman. I send you a million kisses.

Your Karin

13

THE *HENRY GIBBINS*

THERE WERE THINGS I didn't write in my letter to Maman. Even though there was no way I could send the letter to her; and even though she would not get to read it until the war was over; and even though, by that time, when we were all safe and together, it wouldn't matter anymore what I wrote her now—even so, I still couldn't bear to write things that might upset her.

Such as, the ocean was dangerous. It was a battle-field. We might be attacked at any time by German U-boats—submarines.

Our ship was in a convoy of ships. Everywhere I looked, in every direction, there were ships—troopships and cargo ships and sleek, fast destroyers. We had heard that two of the ships in the convoy held nothing but German prisoners. POWs. They were going to America, too. The same people who wanted to kill us because we were Jews. Sometimes I dreamed about those people. Nightmares, in which they came tramping onto the *Henry Gibbins*—only sometimes it was the attic room at Madame Zetain's. Once I woke up moaning, and Jo reached up and held my hand so I could go back to sleep.

It took seventeen days to cross the ocean, and on nearly every one of those days, there was a U-boat alert. Those submarines scared me more than anything, the way they hid in the sea like sharks. To confuse them, our ships zigzagged and poured out smoke like fog to hide us. We had guns, too, and bombs the sailors dropped over the sides of the ships.

The third night we were at sea, I was brushing my teeth in the washroom when the alarm bells went off, clanging and clanging. I ran out into the corridor and up to the deck. Everybody was shouting and rushing around. Marc found me and we stayed together.

Clouds of smoke rose around the ships. The sailors got the lifeboats ready. Then the all-clear bell rang.

People were saying we'd been attacked by U-boats.

No, we had gone through minefields. No, it had been a false alarm. No, there had been a fire. No, no fire; it was a smoke screen, and the destroyers had driven off the U-boats. Nobody really knew.

Days on the deck were never quiet, either. The engines, the ocean, the wind. Nothing still. The sun burned. People made shade with an umbrella, a piece of cardboard, a bit of canvas. A soldier gave Marc a shirt that we roped up like an awning. I'd sit under it and listen to the people talking and singing in Spanish, Greek, French, Yiddish, Italian, Slovak, Serbo-Croatian. It sounded like every language in the world.

"Eighteen languages," Marc said. He always seemed to know facts like that. He went around listening to everyone, trying out words, trying to learn every language. He claimed he had already spoken to at least half of the people on the boat.

Before, he had always been the quiet one, the solitary one, the one with his nose in a book. Now we had reversed places.

I liked to sit by myself in the stern of the ship and look back toward Europe and Maman. The wind blew, it never stopped. On either side, in the distance, I saw other ships. I felt the engines working and watched the ship rise out of the waves and fall back in. Marc would come looking for me. "Why are you back here all alone? Don't always be by yourself."

But I didn't mind it. I felt different from everyone, separate from their happiness at going to America. Marc worried about me. It made me love him more, but I still went off to be by myself, to watch the wake widen and disappear behind us.

14

ON THE OCEAN

THE AMERICAN LADY, Ruth Gruber, set up a blackboard on the deck, and every day we sat in front of it to learn useful American talk, like "Where is the post office?" and "Please open the window." I loved looking at her. She was so bright, like a painting. I tried to draw her, but the picture was no good. It didn't resemble her at all. I ended up throwing it away.

"Maybe I'll never be an artist," I said to Marc. We paced back and forth on the deck. And I thought, *artist*. It seemed so long ago that I'd dreamed about that, and so seriously.

"At least you're learning English," Marc said.

"I don't see what that's got to do with it."

"No...I suppose not. Just something useful, I meant." He sounded listless, not really interested. His skin was sort of greenish around his mouth.

"Are you sick?" I said. "Getting seasick, after all this time?" I wondered if he'd gotten skinnier, even with all the food. "Chow time" was what the soldiers called meals and "chowing down" was what they called eating. Sometimes, though, neither of us ate much, because the ship was always moving and the food slid around, and you'd just lose your appetite.

Even so, Marc had grown taller again, at least another inch. He looked older, too. He had a little mustache, but he'd had that for a while. He was fourteen, so it was no surprise. I was taller, too, and had grown little breasts. About those—it seemed as if one day I was just as usual, flat, and then the next day, there they were.

Suddenly I had one of those frightening thoughts that entered my mind and wouldn't leave. What if Maman didn't recognize us when she saw us again? What if we'd changed so much she didn't even know we were her own children?

"Marc, is that possible?"

"What?" He looked at me blankly.

"I was thinking...Maman, when she sees us again...I'm afraid...Will she know us?"

"Yes," he said.

"Are you sure?"

"Yes!" He was so irritable I should have stopped, but I didn't.

"Marc, look at us. What if we've changed so much that—"

"Don't be absurd," he said. "Talk about something else."

"I don't want to talk about something else. This is what I'm thinking about. Oh, okay," I said in English, seeing that I was really annoying him. "Okay, okay." Then, in French, trying to be more agreeable, I asked, "Who did you talk to today?"

"Nobody."

"Nobody? I don't believe it. Not you."

He shrugged. "Just some old guy who was in Valence, too. He's a doctor. Doesn't have anything left, not even a pair of shoes."

"Valence? You met somebody who was in Valence? Did he know Monsieur Taubert—and Maman, did he know her?"

"Hey! Take it easy!" English again. That was what the soldiers said when they wanted someone to calm down. He leaned over the railing.

"Did you ask him about Maman?"

"He didn't say anything about her."

I stood next to him, disappointed. The sun was going down, a hot blur on the horizon. For just a moment, I had hoped there was someone here who might have seen Maman. It would have been so good. Someone who could say, *Oh, yes. Your mother—she's fine now! Monsieur is keeping her safe.*

I focused on remembering Maman—her face, her eyes, exactly how she had looked that last day, lying on the couch.

My mind drifted, and I tried to remember the last time I'd seen Grand-mère. Four years ago, that night... And Papa, before they took him away to Drancy, where they had kept all the men before they put them on the trains. It was getting harder to recall the color of Papa's eyes, and to see the tiny C-shaped scar above his eyebrow that I had always liked to touch.

"Marc, what if I forget what Maman looks like? I couldn't bear it."

"Stop. You go from one thing to another. First, Maman won't recognize us. Then, you won't remember her. You just make yourself unhappy."

"But, Marc—"

"No," he said. "I don't want to talk about this. It's not good for us."

I leaned against him, my back against his back. The wind had died down. Little waves rippled the surface of the water. Maybe he was right. Better not to think about Maman. Better to think about other things. About where we were going. The huge, huge country of America. The soldiers had tacked up pictures in the cafeteria. Movie stars and city streets. Esther Williams in a white bathing suit. The lighted city of New York. The Statue of Liberty.

I felt proud of us, of all we'd been through and how we stayed together and helped each other. I tried to think of other good things, of what lay ahead. Safety, no more war, food all the time.

But all I could really think was that I wanted to be home again. In France. On rue Erlanger, in our own apartment. I wanted Maman. I wanted Papa. And Grand-mère. I wanted everyone. Everything. I wanted my life as it used to be.

And I couldn't have it. It was gone.

15

An American Moon

THE TRAIN ROCKED through the night. Next to me, Marc dozed on the green plush seat, an American newspaper in his lap. The car was jammed with people sleeping, arms flung out, legs in the aisle.

I couldn't get comfortable. My mind kept traveling from Maman in Valence, to the truck that had taken us over the mountains, to the old wreck of a bicycle crashing on the hill, and then suddenly I'd see myself crouching near the cave and hear Maria Theresa saying, *Go to Naples!*

And we had, and they had taken us on the ship, and we had come, at last, seventeen days later, safely into New York Harbor. I saw the Statue of Liberty in the moonlight. A full moon, and Lady Liberty holding up her torch. She was French like us, made in France more than fifty years ago. Maman had told us all about it.

But the moon was American, I thought. It looked different from our French moon, fatter and more golden.

We had stayed on the ship overnight. When we left, they gave us tags to pin on our clothes. U.S. ARMY CASUAL BAGGAGE.

"As if we're packages," I said, when Marc translated.

"It's because we're not official. I guess they don't know what to call us."

"How about *visitors*? Aren't we guests of President Roosevelt? We're not here to stay."

They had put us on a ferry to New Jersey, then taken us to the train station in a city called Hoboken. The station boomed and echoed with the noise of hundreds of people. All of us, plus soldiers, reporters, and Americans who had come to the station looking for their relatives. I watched enviously as they found aunts, uncles, cousins. They were hugging and crying, saying hello and good-bye at the same time. Was it better to have no one, I wondered, or better to find a relative, someone you loved, and then have to separate? No one could leave our group, not even those with relatives right here to take them in. We weren't prisoners, not like those German POWs, but we weren't free, either.

On the train, I wanted to sleep, but I was too restless. Too scared, too excited. We were on our way to Fort Ontario, in the city of Oswego, state of New York. *Ahhs-wee-go.* Funny word. How about *Rose-a-velt*? Another funny word. Some people said, "Rooos-a-velt." Which was correct?

In the middle of this thought, I did fall asleep, and I entered a dream so real I could see every leaf on the trees. I was walking with Maman in a park. It was a spring night. The moon was almost too bright. Maman's hair smelled of roses. "Rose-a-velt, Maman," I said, and she laughed, happy at my joke.

Then I was awake again, as fast as I'd fallen asleep. The train rounded a curve, and through the window I saw the shadowy front of the train, like a long metal snake. We sped past dark little houses and dark stretches of empty land. So much land, so much space. And no damage. I'd noticed that right away. Everything here was perfect—and large: buildings, trains, people. Even the smiles were bigger. All the Americans smiled as if they had extra teeth.

"Marc," I said, "are you awake?"

"No."

"I want to ask you something. Are you happy?"

"No."

"Unhappy?"

"No."

"What are you?"

"Sleeping. Trying to."

"I am," I said.

"What, happy? That's good."

"No. The other."

His eyes flickered open. "Sorry," he said, and he covered my hand with his.

As the darkness peeled away, I saw big flat fields, clumps of houses, trees. The sun came up. The train hooted, three long hoots. All at once, a murmur went through the car. "Oswego...Oswego..." Marc and I put our faces to the dusty window. The train rolled past houses, a road, a field, and then water spreading to the horizon. Lake Ontario—it was like an ocean. Even the lakes here were bigger than our lakes in France.

Then we saw fences, high metal fences topped with barbed wire. Everyone fell silent, until someone cursed. It sounded almost like crying. A curse, and then, "Barbed wire..."

The wheels thumped. The train slowed to a stop. We were here.

16

THE EIGHTH LIFE

WE SAT ON the train and waited. We talked to the people sitting behind us, two older girls named Reva and Dani, and Dani's father. The girls were cousins and had escaped from Hungary by passing themselves off as Christians. By a miracle, Dani said, she had found her father in Italy.

It was stuffy in the train, even with the windows open. A hot breeze blew in. We were given cookies and milk, handed in through the open windows. There were soldiers everywhere, waiting as we got off the train, and reporters and photographers.

We were crushed together, milling around on a

grassy field, surging one way, then another. It was all noise and heat and questions and confusion. I stayed close to Marc. We lined up in front of a long row of tables. Soldiers sat behind the tables, wearing arm-bands with big white letters: MP.

The air shimmered with heat. Outside the barbed-wire fence, people from the town were lined up, staring at us. Hands gripped the fence, eyes watched us.

"Hey! Hi!" A man in a rumpled gray suit spoke in English to Marc. "How are you two kids doing?" He stood very close, talking too fast. Marc had to translate for me. "He's a reporter, and he wants to know how it feels to be free. What do you want to tell him?" Marc said in French.

"Good, of course. Does he think it feels bad?"

Marc spoke in English. "Very good. Thank you. We both say the same. My sister and I, pleased to be in this country."

"Great, son! Thanks!" The reporter scribbled on a pad, then moved to another person.

A moment later, a woman wearing a flowery summer dress and carrying an armful of toys handed me a rubber doll. The doll wore a red rubber dress, little blue rubber shoes, and a red rubber ribbon in her rubber hair.

I looked at Marc, and he said, "She says it's a welcome-to-America gift for you."

"I'm too old for dolls," I said.

"Karin, don't be rude. Thank her."

"Swell," I said in English. "Thanks, GI Joe!"

The woman smiled, then looked at my bare feet and patted my cheek.

The soldier sitting behind the table said, "Wazyrname?"

"Pardon?" Marc said.

"Wazyrname, buddy? Name. Name," he said loudly.

Marc started speaking in French. "*Je m'appelle* Marc Levi—" I poked him, and he began again. "I am Marc Levi and this is my—"

"Lasname first, buddy."

What was he saying now? I got the *buddy* part. That was like *kid*. Another friendly American word.

"Levi Marc," Marc said. He looked at me and grinned a little. "Levi Karin."

"Levi, Marc. Levi, Karin," the soldier said.

They were saying our names backward. Was this an American custom I was going to have to learn? "Levi Karin," I whispered to myself, trying to get used to it.

The soldier winked at me. "Okay, kids, we're in good shape." He held out a slip of paper with a number on it. "Here's your room assignment, but you better get some food first." He pointed. "The mess hall is that way."

Our room was in an army barracks, a long two-story wooden building. We walked down a dimly lit hallway, carrying the towels and soap we'd been issued, and found our door halfway to the end. Our names were on the door, as if we belonged here!

The room had two cots, a table, two chairs, and some shelves. Sheets and a blanket were folded at the bottom of each cot. I put the doll on the table, then went to the window and looked out. I sat in one chair, then got up and sat in the other.

"Are they comfortable?" Marc asked. He was laughing at me.

"Fine."

"Not 'fine.' Wonderful! Look at this room, Karin. Don't you like it?"

I looked all around again, up at the ceiling and down at the floor. I went around and touched the walls. "Yes. I like it."

I told myself, of course I liked it; this was our new home. We were going to live here. Live in this room.

Marc bounced on one cot, then the other. "Both the same. Both comfortable. Which side of the room do you want?"

"You choose."

Marc pointed. "Your side. And over here, mine. We'll put the table in the middle." He pushed his cot to one side.

I flapped out a sheet and spread it over my cot. If Maman were here, she'd say, *Make it smooth, darling*. I pulled the sheet tight at the corners. I kept repeating to myself, *This room is my new home. This is where I live now. This is my new life.* But which life was it? I was like a cat with nine lives. The first life—my real life, the happy one—had been in Paris, on rue Erlanger.

Then came the second life—still in Paris, but without Grand-mère or Papa—when the world looked the same but had changed in every way.

My third life was in the attic room in Madame Zetain's house, and the fourth was the weeks after we left there. What did I remember of that life? Not much, except sleeping in fields, where stones poked into my back.

The fifth life was with Monsieur Taubert and Uncle Leo, Bernard, and Simone. If Maman hadn't been so sick, if the Germans hadn't come, it would almost have been a good life. Darling Monsieur Taubert. I missed him, too. The sixth life was in Italy with Marc, a life that took me away, and away, and away from Maman. And the seventh life was on the *Henry Gibbins*, which took me even farther away.

Now I was beginning another life, the eighth one. But not the last. That could only be when we were with Maman again.

17

THE FENCE

SOMETHING STRANGE happened those first weeks in Fort Ontario. Marc became Maman. And I became something else, but I didn't know what, exactly. I was Karin Levi or Levi Karin, but that was only my name, and the rest of me—I couldn't tell. It was as if I'd gotten lost somewhere.

But about Marc: He had traded the shirt the soldier gave him on the boat for an alarm clock. And now we lived by that clock. He kept it on the floor next to his cot. *Ticktock...ticktock...ticktock.* It rang every morning to wake us up. It told us to get dressed. It told us when to take a walk and when to go to the mess hall to eat.

"We have to keep a routine," Marc said. He made us do exercises, the same bending and touching our toes we used to do in the attic room. We had to study at a certain time. And read. And practice our English.

That's what I mean about Marc's being Maman.

It wasn't that I minded doing those things. It was his attitude. He wanted to be in control of everything. In control of me. In control of time. In control of his clock. I couldn't even touch it. He was afraid I'd drop it. He was even more afraid that I'd overwind it.

He had also acquired an American dictionary, and he was devoted to it. It was a soft-covered military edition. He let me use it, but he watched me every moment. "Don't ever lick your thumb and turn the page," he said.

"Why would I do that?"

"Just don't."

"But why would I even want to? Did you see me lick my thumb?"

"Don't argue with me," he said.

But I wanted to argue with him. More and more, about everything. There was something about the way he said things, so sure of himself, so right all the time. We argued about food and "free time"—which was time when we weren't together—and we argued about the quarantine. Marc hated it.

For the first month, everyone in the fort except the Americans was in quarantine. We couldn't leave the fort. Soldiers were posted at the entrances to keep us in and to keep everyone else out. They said it was for health and administrative reasons.

"Whatever that means," Marc said. "They stuff us in here like sardines, or pigs in a pen. What happened to free America? Why did we come here, if we're put behind barbed wire?"

"We're not in jail," I argued. "We can go wherever we want, we can do what we want. Nobody stops us."

"Go where we want? I want to go to Aunt Hannah in California. Can I do that? No. Is that being free? Is it being free to live with barbed wire? With soldiers everywhere?"

"The wire's just there," I said. "It doesn't mean anything."

"Don't talk without thinking, Karin," Marc said. "Of course it means something. Everything means something. Nothing is accidental. And tell me, how do you think someone like Mrs. Stein feels seeing that barbed wire?"

I felt ashamed. I wasn't going to be that stupid and

say barbed wire wouldn't bother Mrs. Stein, who had been in a concentration camp.

"Marc," I said, "remember Papa's gold tooth?"

"Papa didn't have a gold tooth."

"He did so, right here." I pointed to my mouth.

"You're wrong."

"No, I'm not!"

"Well, I don't care. Just stop talking about it."

"But I want to talk about it. Once I asked him who kept that tooth so shiny, and he said it was the little gold workers. He told me a whole story about it, and I was so young I believed every word."

Marc got up abruptly.

"I wanted to see those little gold polishers. Whenever he took a nap, I'd watch him, hoping his mouth would open, and I'd catch one of them doing his job."

"Why are you always thinking about things that are done with, Karin? It only makes you feel weak and unhappy."

"No, it doesn't," I said.

"Does it make you feel strong and happy?"

I looked down. Why wouldn't he let me talk about Papa's gold tooth? Was it a crime to think about home and things I knew? Was it a crime to want to talk in a normal way?

The truth was, I didn't feel normal. We were kept in, fenced in, barbed-wired in. Us, only us—so what did that make us? If the normal world was right there, right before our eyes, on the other side of the fence—houses, trees, kids, cars, bikes—then what were we on our side? Abnormal? Freaks?

I didn't have anything—not clothes, not money, not a home, not a family. One day, a man in a suit had stopped at the fence. His shoes were so polished I saw the reflection of trees in them. He had his son with him, a boy about my age. The boy didn't say a word. I stared at him, and he stared back. He couldn't tell from looking at me that once I'd been like him. Once I'd had my own bedroom in my own home, and my parents worked and had respect, and I had food and love.

Sometimes I wanted to shout at people like that, people from town who came to the fence and stared, as if we were strange animals. But I didn't. I didn't say anything. I only tried not to feel that way. But that was why, for a while, I hated going near the fence.

Dearest Maman,

Marc has gone out for a walk. I try not to write to you when he's around, because he gets upset. He doesn't like me to notice this, but I do. I think he misses you so much, Maman, that it's hard for him to even talk about you. I understand, but I can't be like that. Writing you is like talking to you, and if I didn't do it, I don't know what I would do.

I want to tell you about some new friends we've made. Their names are Elisabeth and George Stein. They are both sort of short, tubby people. I hope you don't think that's rude of me, to talk about them that way!

Marc and I met them one morning on one of our walks around the camp. Mr. Stein was picking up trash with a pointed stick and putting it into a paper bag that Mrs. Stein was carrying. A lot of the men here do maintenance work. This was the first time I saw a woman doing it, too. I said, in English, "Hello. Good morning. Is that much fun?"

Mr. Stein answered in German. "It's quite pleasant, my child."

Mrs. Stein translated into French. She made a telescope with her hands, looked up into the sky, and said, "This is even more fun. Do you enjoy stargazing?" And her face got all pink because, it seems, she is very shy. I never thought a grown-up could be so shy!

"A telescope?" I said. "I always wanted to look at the stars and the planets and the sky and everything through a telescope." I spoke in French because she understands it perfectly.

Then Mr. Stein lifted his stick like a bow and pretended to play a violin. "Also, also fun," he said in English, and we all laughed. I thought it was a joke—you know, trash picking, stargazing, violin playing—as if they could do anything, and did.

But it turned out to be no joke. We visited them later in their room. Marc says they're the most interesting people he's ever met. Mrs. Stein was a piano teacher in Vienna, and Mr. Stein was a violinist with the symphony orchestra. And in Europe she did have a telescope. Stargazing was her hobby.

They have one son, Thomas. They sent him to America a long time ago to live with relatives. Now he's an American soldier. They had planned to follow Thomas to *this country sooner, but the Germans arrested Mrs. Stein. They said she was a spy, but Mr. Stein says it was really because she was a Christian married to him, a Jew. She was in a concentration camp for six months before they let her go. He went into hiding.*

Anyway, Maman, now they're here, and I'm glad they're our friends. When I'm with them, I think it's almost like being with Grand-mère and (although I never knew either one of my grandfathers) Grand-père.

Good night, Maman. I love you more than anyone in the world.

Your Karin

18

Fench Club

"Hello! Hi!" a girl said in English to me. We were in the mess hall. It was noisy and crowded as usual. The girl put down her tray and sat next to me. I moved closer to Marc to make room for her.

"Very please to meet you," she said. She took a biscuit, slathered margarine on it, looked first at me, then across me at Marc. "Your name, yes please? I, here, am Eva." She tapped herself on the chest. She looked about Marc's age, maybe a little older. She had a broad face covered with freckles, slanted green eyes like little green fish, and a head of tight curls.

"Karin," I said, pointing to myself. I waited for Marc to introduce himself, but he didn't say a word, just looked down at his plate. So brave, my brother, everywhere except around girls.

I pointed to him, thought for a moment to get the words right, and said in English, "Marc here, he is my brother. Older," I added.

Eva laughed. "Oh, yes, older. And what of this, ah, ah, quarantine, Karin and Marc? I think, phooey!" She leaned across me and blew the last word out in Marc's face. His forehead turned red.

"Does he talk?" Eva whispered loudly. "You guys—" *Guys* was another word the Americans used a lot. "You guys know the fench club?"

"The French club?" Marc said. Now his ears went red, too.

"Fench club! Fench club. You know, at the fench!"

"Oh, *fence*," I said.

"Yes, surely. Fench club. To be friendship from town to us." She leaned across me again. "So. Okay, Mr. Marc?"

Poor Marc dropped his napkin and then a fork.

"Always shy?" Eva said, in her big stage whisper. She gave him a gleaming glance. She asked where we came from. France, I told her. Paris. We were Jewish.

"Ahhhh, ahhhh, Jude," she said. She was Hungarian and Catholic. "Is okay with you?"

"No," Marc said.

"No, not okay?" Her green eyes narrowed.

"Marc!" I said.

Now *he* leaned across me. I felt like a "fench" myself. "A joke, Karin," he said in French. "Is it all right if I make a joke?" And then in English, to Eva, "It is okay. You like us. We like you. Okay, okay! All okay."

"Okay, okay. Okeydokey," she said. "Friends." She stuck out her hand to Marc and then to me.

Volunteers came into the fort to teach us English and other things that would help us get along in America. The soldiers let the volunteers in, even though the quarantine was still on. But some people from inside were going out, too, despite the quarantine. Marc knew some older boys who had gone under the fence one night and hitchhiked to Syracuse. "They didn't get back until after midnight," he said.

I didn't like the way he was smiling, as if he thought they had done a great thing. After that, I kept waking up in the middle of the night and listening for Marc's breathing.

One day, Eva came up to me after English lessons and said, "Okeydokey! Fench club, now, friend! Let's go."

"No, Eva. No. Thank you!"

"Yes, Karin. Welcome very much. Fench club!"

She grabbed my hand, yanked me along. I would have been mad if Marc had done it, but Eva was laughing. At the fence, she started talking to a woman on the other side. People jostled around me. I watched two town boys push a piggy bank through the fence to a boy on our side. I didn't say anything to anyone, but after a while I saw that I had been wrong.

Just like Eva said, "Fench club." People came here to talk any way they could. They used sign language and body language, smiles and a lot of laughing, and presents, too. Town people were passing stuff like toys, clothes, and food through the fence, over the fence, under the fence.

I saw a bureau come over one day. Two big men on the sidewalk lifted it and tipped it over, and two skinny men on our side—one of them with rags tied around his feet—reached up and caught it. They staggered a moment, then got it down safely. *Thump!* The American men clasped their hands over their heads and danced, and our men did the same thing.

Then one of the men on the town side untied his shoes, took them off, and threw them over to the man with rags on his feet.

That man picked up the shoes. He bent over very slowly and picked them up, one at a time. He looked over at the town man, in his socks now, and the town man nodded. The man with rags sat down on the ground and, still slowly, put them on, one at a time, and tied them and stood up. He walked around in the shoes. They were a little too big, but he was smiling, and he was crying.

19

HATING MARC

I KEPT HOPING someone would throw a pair of shoes over the fence to me. I had heard we might go to the American schools when the quarantine was lifted. I couldn't go barefoot! Marc went to the fence almost every day to practice his English, and I went with him to listen and to make sure I'd be there if someone did want to give me shoes.

One day, a woman Marc had talked to before passed a book under the fence. "You said you liked reading." She had a slow, drawling voice. She was pushing a stroller with a little child in it.

"Yes! I like reading. Very much," Marc said.

"That's a good book. Came from my book club."

"How long I may keep it?" Marc asked.

"Oh, it's yours," she said. "I finished it."

I understood almost everything she said. I was getting better at that, especially if people didn't talk too fast. I looked at the book. *"The Grapes of Wath,"* I read out loud.

"Wrath, honey," the woman said. "Not the *w* sound. *Rrrr. Rrrr. Rrrath.* Roll those *r*s, honey."

It was an American habit for people to use sweet names like honey and tootsie, even if they didn't know you very well. Marc stood, smiling and stroking the cover of the book. "Pass it on to someone else when you're done, honey," the woman said.

Marc walked around the rest of the day holding the book. He started reading it that evening, with the dictionary next to him. He'd read a page with the dictionary, then read it again.

The next day, when it rained, Marc said we didn't have to take our walk that day. Too gloomy. We could have a day off from studying. "Vacation time," he called it.

Oh yes, so he could read! But I didn't mind. I had

a book from the camp library called *Daddy-Long-Legs*. It looked hard but interesting. I could have checked out an easier book, but I didn't want Marc to think I was reading baby stuff.

We stayed in our room, reading, the dictionary between us on the table. It was cozy inside. Marc pulled the chain on the light hanging from the ceiling. We read quietly. I wasn't doing too well. I'd work to get a few sentences, and then it would all sort of blur and I'd have to concentrate hard to get a few more sentences.

Suddenly, Marc almost shouted, "This is a magnificent book!"

I looked up. "What's it about?"

"A great story!" He went back to reading.

"Tell me what it is. Tell me the story, Marc. Marc!" I was ready for a break from struggling with my book. It was written as letters from a lonely girl to someone she loved but couldn't see. Almost like me and Maman.

"It's about this tremendously poor family," Marc said. "The Joads. They have to leave their farm because there's no water. Everything's turned to dust. There's a drought and they don't have money and they lose everything."

"You know all that already?" I couldn't believe it. I couldn't have told that much about my book.

"They've got all their stuff piled in their car; they

had to leave their farm—did I say that already?—and they're sleeping on the road, poor but free, and—"

"Who are these people?" I kept my finger in my place, so it wouldn't look as if I was just trying to pass time. "I thought this was an American story."

"It is. They have poor people here, too."

"No, they don't."

"Karin, poor people are here, just like everywhere. John Steinbeck, the author of this book, is probably a genius. Everything he writes is so real. The people are so real. You feel as if you know them and everything's happening to you."

"I'll read it, when I finish mine," I said.

"No, no, no." He shook his head. "It has scenes that are too mature for you, and besides, you don't have the vocabulary for it."

"Why do you talk to me like that?" I dropped my book. "You talk as if I'm a child!"

"I didn't say that. But you are only—"

"Don't tell me *only*. I'm twelve. I've been through as much as you."

"All right." He started reading again.

"'All right' what? Don't say things just to make me feel better! You don't mean it. I know you don't mean it! You order me around all the time; you're always making up rules." I picked up the rubber doll and threw her on the floor. "I hate you, Marc! I hate your rules! I hate your clock!"

"I don't know what's the matter with you," he said. I wanted him to shout back, but he kept his voice even. "I'm trying to take care of us. Of you. Like Maman said I should." He bent down, picked up the doll, and put her on the table between us. "I'm just trying to do things right," he said.

I didn't know why I'd yelled. If Maman had heard me—the thought made me ashamed. "I know you're trying to help me," I mumbled.

He propped up his book. "So are we friends again?"

After a moment, I nodded.

"Say it," he said.

"What?"

"Say we're friends again."

"Marc..."

"No, say it."

"All right. We're friends again."

"Good," he said. "Still hate my clock?"

20

SOUNDING AMERICAN

"HI, HI!" A BLOND, freckled girl was waving from the other side of the fence.

"Hello," I said.

She tapped her chest, the way Eva had the first day we met. "Me, Peggy Bradbury. Who you?"

"I am Karin Levi. Twelve years old. I have a brother. Do you have a brother? Or maybe a sister?"

"Huh!" She twisted her ponytail. "You can speak English good." She had a pudgy nose and big brown eyes. She took a small chocolate bar from her pocket and poked it through the fence to me.

"Swell! Thank you," I said. "Hubba-hubba!" I knew enough now not to add "GI Joe." I broke off a piece of chocolate and pushed the rest back toward her.

She shook her head. "No, Karin. Keep it!"

"Keep it? Sure?" I said.

"Yes!"

"Swell!" I put it in my pocket. "Thank you once and twice!"

"Don't say 'once and twice,' Karin. You want to sound American?"

"Oh yes, please."

"Okay. Say, 'Thanks again!'"

"'Thanks again!'"

"Good." She smiled. "Know what these are?" She pointed to her feet. "Sneakers! Can you say that?"

"'Sneakers,'" I repeated, to be polite. I knew that word. I wanted a pair for myself.

Peggy pointed to her heavy, dark blue pants. She wore them rolled at the ankles. "Dun-ga-rees," she said.

"'Dun-ga-rees.'" I wanted a pair of them, too.

Peggy pointed to her nose.

"The nose," I said quickly. I touched my hair and said, "The hair." I touched my mouth. "The mouth." My eyes. My chin. My arms. My feet. The sky. The trees.

"Wow," Peggy said. "That's swell!"

I pointed to the sun and then behind me to the lake. To the barracks and the fence and the grass and the windows in the barracks, and I said all those words.

"You know a lot of stuff," Peggy said.

"You are correct. I am trying all the time."

"Don't say 'You are correct,' Karin. It sounds drippy."

"'Drippy'?" That was a new one for me.

"You know. Dopey, dumb, dumbo!"

I shook my head. I didn't understand.

"Stupid!"

"Oh. Stupid."

"Well, not exactly. But sort of." She wrinkled her nose. "When you agree, say, 'You got it!'"

"'You got it.'"

"No. Say it like this, Karin." Peggy snapped her fingers. "You *got* it!"

"'You *got* it!'"

"That's it. Swell!"

"Swell!" I echoed.

"And don't say 'Hello,' when you meet someone. Say 'Hi.'"

"'Hi.'"

She shook her head. "More jazzy, Karin. Like this. '*Hiii. Hiii*, Peggy!'"

"'*Hiii. Hiii*, Peggy!'"

"Super, Karin. You sound just like anyone, like a real American. Want to be friends?"

"Yes, okay," I said.

"Super!"

Dearest Maman,

I have so much to tell you. The Red Cross got in touch with Aunt Hannah in Del Rey, California, and told her we were here. She wrote to us right away, the best letter! She said if the doctor allows her to travel such a long distance—she has a bad heart—she'll come and visit us. She doesn't know yet when that will be. But imagine this: It takes five whole days and nights by train to cross this country just one way, and

21

TRUDI AND MARIKA

"ARE YOU COMING with me?" Marc asked. He was rubbing Vaseline in his hair to smooth it down and make it shine.

I covered my notebook with my arm. "No, not tonight. You go." There was a sing-along in the big hall, but I wanted to stay in and finish my letter to Maman.

"Tomas is going to sing solo," Marc said. "Don't you want to hear him?" Tomas was Marc's age, short and handsome. "I know you like him," Marc added.

Now I was sure I wouldn't go.

"What are you writing, anyway?"

"Nothing." I got up and put my notebook under my pillow.

"Tomas is serious about his voice. He wants an audience. I promised I'd bring anybody I could."

"'Anybody'?" I sat down on the cot and fussed with the rubber doll. I'd finally given her a name, an American name: Betty Lou. "'Anybody' is who I am? You can't promise me like that to someone else. I'm not a dog."

"Don't get dramatic, Karin. Come on, you'll have fun." He picked up Betty Lou. "Tell her to come," he said to the doll. He pestered me until I agreed.

"Remember to clap good and loud for Tomas," he said as we walked over.

"What if he's a bad singer and I don't want to clap for him?"

"Clap anyway."

"That's so fake, Marc!"

"Sometimes it's better to be good to your friends than worry about being pristine." He waited. He knew I didn't know what *pristine* meant, but I wasn't about to ask.

Inside, there were rows of folding chairs. Marc found a seat with friends in the first row. I sat down next to a blond girl with thick bangs, who stammered out her name. "T-Trudi." Beside her was a girl with a ribbon in her dark hair, and a little pointed face. She said something in Greek. What I caught was her name: Marika.

The singing began. An older boy played the piano. The lyrics of American songs were flashed up on a screen, with a bouncing ball beneath the words to help us keep the place. We all especially loved one American song called "Don't Fence Me In," about being free to go anywhere under the stars. It was practically the Fort Ontario theme song. Land, freedom, no fences. Especially no fences.

Later, Tomas, wearing a fedora and suspenders, soloed. A Spanish song. His friends shouted and whistled. I saw Marc on his feet, cheering. Maman, I thought, would be surprised to see him so boisterous.

After Tomas came the real surprise. Trudi sang, and she had a great big voice that went right down my spine. Marika and I looked at each other and smiled proudly, as if we were the ones responsible.

"Glad you went?" Marc asked later. He knew I was. He just wanted to hear me say that he had been right.

22

THE BIKE RIDE

I WAS RICH in friends. Eva, Peggy, Mr. and Mrs. Stein, and now Marika and Trudi. It had been years since I'd had friends my own age. I hardly even remembered how to act like a friend, but I pretended I did. I was never sure I was doing it right. Marika, Trudi, and I were all Jewish, all twelve years old, and we all talked only about *now*. No sorrows. No sad stories. No speaking about anything that had happened to us, to our families before we came to the United States.

Our friendship was a happy one, an American friendship.

We learned to call the big hall the "rec" hall, and on Friday nights, we went there for movies. We walked around the fort together, arms linked, singing and talking. We scooted under a break in the fence and swam in the lake. No bathing suits. We went in wearing our clothes, then dried out in the sun and the wind.

When Jewish women from a city called Rochester brought boxes of clothes to the fort, the three of us went together and picked out wardrobes for each other. I got sneakers and dungarees, a blue dress called a jumper, two blouses, and a sweater. Now I was rich in clothes.

We talked about going to school again. We were all a little nervous about it. None of us had been in a real school for a long time. Trudi was afraid she was too far behind and would never catch up.

"Oh no, forget that," Marika said. She wanted to go to school, she said, because "I really, really true like American boys."

Trudi began singing, her way of going past nervousness. "'Who is Sylv...iaaa,'" she sang, "'that all the swains adore her?'" She remembered the words to all the songs we sang in the rec hall.

"'Swains'?" Marika said. "What is it?"

Trudi shook her head and kept singing.

"Pigs," I said. "You know." I made pig sounds.

Marika's pointy chin quivered as she tried not to laugh. "'Pigs,' Karin?"

"Pigs," I said firmly, the way Marc would.

"'All the pigs adore her,'" Marika sang. "Sure. Okay." We all sang it together. "'Who is Sylv...iaaaa, that all the *pigs* adore her?'" Our arms were linked, we almost harmonized, and we kept breaking into laughter. I couldn't help thinking we were acting just the way friends would—just like regular American kids.

One day Marika and I went to the fence, so I could listen to the people and so she could boy spot. A few minutes later, I saw Peggy across the street. She was riding a bike. I called to her. "Peggy! Hiii, Peggy."

She hopped off the bike and walked it across the street. "Hi, Karin!"

I introduced her to Marika. "Beauty bike, Piggy," Marika said.

"Peggy," Peggy corrected. "Short *e* sound, Marika. Like this. E*h*. Eh, eh, eh. Peggy."

"'Eh, eh, eh.' Piggy," Marika said.

Peggy laughed. "You guys want to ride my bike for a while?" She tried to lift it over the fence.

A man in a plaid shirt helped. "Catch, girls," he said to me and Marika, and we managed to grab the bike before it fell.

"For us, true, Piggy?" Marika said, holding the handlebars.

"Yes," Peggy said. "Go ahead, get on. Ride it."

"I cannot," Marika said. "No knowledge of bike."

"What about you, Karin?"

I had never ridden a two-wheel bike, but I wanted to try. Papa had bicycled to work every day. I straddled the bike. I liked the feeling of the rubber grips on the handlebars. The moment I put my feet on the pedals, I started to fall.

"Balance yourself, Karin," Peggy said.

I tried again, but the bike kept tipping. Marika held the seat, and I pushed off. The bike wobbled. Marika let go. I kept pedaling, wobbling but not falling. I was riding, almost flying. The wind rushed past my face. I never wanted to stop.

Dearest Maman,

Today, in the mail, we got a check for thirty dollars from Aunt Hannah! Mr. Stein said an American man has to work almost two weeks to earn that much money. Aunt Hannah said to spend it on anything we need. Marc and I are both a little dizzy with so much money all for ourselves. That's not all, either. She said she wants us to come live with her! She's all alone in her house and has plenty of room.

When I think that Aunt Hannah knew Papa as a little boy and that he was her favorite nephew (she said so in her letter), I already love her. If only we could go to her and stay with her until the war is over, but we can't. None of us is allowed to live anywhere except right here, in Fort Ontario.

At least the quarantine is over. We still have to show our blue passes to go out and come back in, plus we children can't be away from the fort for more than three hours at a time. The grown-ups can go away for six hours, but they can't go more than thirty miles, and everyone has to be back by ten o'clock at night. I never saw Mr. Stein angry before. He said it's humiliating to be treated like a child and told when to come and go and for how long. I guess a lot of the adults feel the way he does.

Even so, celebrating the end of the quarantine made yesterday like a big holiday. Practically the whole town of Oswego crowded in to see us. People had relatives visiting from all over the United States. My friend Marika's uncle came from Chicago. Mr. and Mrs. Stein's son, Thomas, hitchhiked from Fort Dix, in New Jersey. If only Aunt Hannah could have been here, but her doctor wouldn't give her permission to travel so far.

Mr. and Mrs. Stein's son was in his army uniform, with his cap tucked into a strap on his shoulder. He is very tall and handsome. Mrs. Stein couldn't stop smiling and patting his arm. She said, "I sent away a boy, and here I have a man returned to me."

My fence friend, Peggy, found me in the crowd and said she wanted to see where we lived. I took her to our room. She looked all around. She looked at my doll, Betty Lou, on my bed, at Marc's books, and at our clothes hanging on the hooks on the wall. "You don't have anything," she said. "Our neighbor says all of you here have new refrigerators, and stoves, too. My dad told her she was wrong, but she wouldn't even listen."

So, Maman, my first month in America is over. Now I can tell you: For a while, I was miserable. I'm much better. I'm used to being here. I have friends, and we're going to be allowed to go to school soon. Plus, I know <u>this is temporary and I'll come home to you</u>. Those are the good things.

But, Maman, I have to say there's still something… like a dark place in my mind. Like a spot, or maybe it's more like a tiny ticking, a sort of pulse that goes <u>bip-bip-bip-bip</u>….I don't know what that is. I don't even know if I'm explaining it right. Sometimes I wake up feeling sick, as if I'd had a nightmare. Or sometimes I'm walking and I have to stop because this feeling comes. Just a bad feeling. I think it's missing you. But sometimes it feels even worse than that.

Maman, I keep all my letters to you in my notebook under my pillow. One day, when we're together again, I'll give them to you, and we'll sit and read them, and I know that bad feeling will be gone. All that will be left will be happiness.

Darling Maman, good night. Sweet, sweet dreams. Your Karin

23

SCHOOL: DAY ONE

ON THE FIRST DAY that we fort children went to school, a huge crowd of adults came to the gate to see us off and give us advice. "Work hard." "Listen to the teachers." "Be respectful." Mrs. Stein fussed over me, smoothing my hair and straightening the collar of my blouse.

Marc was going with Tomas, Eva, and the other teenagers on a bus to the high school. Marika, Trudi, and I were going to Fitzhugh Park Junior High. We showed our passes and went through the gate. The wind blew off the lake. The sky was cloudy.

"Karin and Marika," Trudi said, "I don't want school. I feel sick in the stomach."

"Oooh. Not me," Marika said. But she kept licking her lips. My lips were dry, too.

Worried that we'd be late, we walked fast, checking street signs at every corner. Then, we were afraid that we'd be too early, and we slowed down.

Just as the school came into sight, Trudi bent toward me and whispered, "Karin, I'm too stupid. Too, too stupid!"

"No, Trudi, you're not. You're smart."

She shook her head. She did look sick. I held her hand, and we went up the steps. We all stayed close. American boys and girls were everywhere, all of them holding armfuls of books.

"Hello, girls." A teacher was waiting for us in the front hall. "I'm Mrs. Foster. Welcome to our school." She asked our names and marked them off on her clipboard, then sent us up the stairs to a seventh-grade classroom.

When we walked in, all I could see at first was a blur of people. Then I saw Peggy, sharpening a pencil. She sat down at a desk near the windows. Trudi and Marika had found seats in back. I sat at a desk near Peggy. I was wearing my jumper and had pulled my hair into a pony-tail like her. I don't think she recognized me.

"Hi. I'm Karin," I said. "From the fort."

"Karin! Wow. This is swell! You're here in my class. Super!" She turned to another girl and said, "Zoey! This is the girl from the fort I've been telling you about. She's in our class!"

"Oh, yeah?" Zoey said. Her eyes flicked over me. "What's her name?"

"Karin," Peggy said. "I told you. Karin Levi. She's learning English."

"Well, la-di-da," Zoey said.

Everyone in the room stared at me. I put my new notebook and pencil on the desk.

The teacher walked in. She was tall and wore her hair in rolls at the side of her face. "That's Mrs. Druthy," Peggy whispered. I stood up quickly, the way you should when a teacher enters.

"Yes, what is it?" Mrs. Druthy said, sitting down at her desk and looking at me. "Do you want something?"

I looked around. Marika and Trudi were also standing, but we were the only ones.

"You're the new girls from the fort, aren't you? Which one are you?" Mrs. Druthy said to me.

"Pardon?"

"Your name, dear."

"Karin Levi."

"Do you want something, Karin? No? Then you should sit down. And you, too, girls."

Mrs. Druthy rapped on the desk. "Attention, class!" She made some announcements, then everyone stood for the Pledge of Allegiance.

I put my hand on my heart like everyone else, and I looked at the American flag in the corner of the room, but I didn't say the words. I didn't think I should, because I wasn't an American.

Mrs. Druthy took attendance, calling out each name and then making a mark in her book. She pronounced my last name "Leevee," but that was pretty close. She had more trouble pronouncing Trudi's and Marika's last names.

Suddenly a bell rang. It sounded like the U-boat alert that had sent us all running to the lifeboats. My stomach clenched. But the Americans just started talking and gathering their books. The room was empty in moments.

Mrs. Druthy motioned for me to come to her desk. "You, too, Trudi and Marika," she said. "This is your schedule, girls. You should learn it." She gave us each a card with the time and room number for each class.

No one had told us that students went from classroom to classroom, while the teachers remained at their desks. In France, the students stayed in one room, while the teachers had the freedom of the hall.

"In my country, also," Marika said.

"Me, too," Trudi said. She was pale and taking deep breaths.

Peggy was waiting for us in the hall. "Karin, I'll take you and your girlfriends to your next class. Let me see your cards. Where do you go? What room?"

"Thank you," I said gratefully. "I mean, *thanks!* This is so, you know, hard on the head, very messy for the head."

Peggy nodded. "Yeah, it's confusing. Coming here from sixth grade, I felt the same way my first day."

We followed her down the corridor, up another staircase, and around a corner. She stopped in front of a room. "Math class is here. I have music now. Gotta go! See you later."

After that, we were on our own. We took most classes together, but not all. Somehow, we got through the day, hurrying down corridors, checking numbers on the doors, and doing our best to remember which staircase led where.

24

KARIN,
FIGHTING GIRL

WHEN MARC AND I were together, we spoke French. We said everything we wanted without hesitation. I dreamed in French, too. But Trudi, Marika, and I had our own way of speaking, a mixture of Greek, French, Italian, and American. I always spoke American with Peggy, of course.

"Your accent is so cute," Peggy said. But not everyone thought so, especially Peggy's friend Zoey, who gave me long freezing looks.

Sometimes I made funny mistakes, sometimes stupid ones. One day I read a composition out loud in English class. "My brother, Marc, is my best fiend."

"Stupid or funny, Peggy?" I asked afterward.

"Stupid," Zoey said.

"Shut up, Zoey," Peggy said. "It's funny, Karin. Everybody laughed."

"At me."

"No! Don't be so sensitive." She grabbed me in a hug. "It's okay. We think it's cute!"

Everything was easier around Peggy. With other people, I had to concentrate more, work harder to get things right. Sometimes I couldn't find the words I wanted, or I'd find the wrong ones. I knew I was as quick as anyone else, but that didn't always help me.

Some boys followed Marika and me home one day, mimicking the way we talked. Marika flirted with them. "Cute boys," she called out. "What you say, cute boys?"

"Stupid boys," I said. I remembered jumping on the back of the boy who had attacked Marc in the hills in Italy. I didn't want Marika to speak to the boys or even look at them. I showed her my hand in a fist.

"What, Karin, fighting girl? No!" she said. "The boys like this teasing, they like to see so mad a girl."

Trudi wasn't with us. She had been put back into third grade, in the elementary school. She was embarrassed and cried a lot. Marika and I tried to comfort her. We kept telling her she was as smart as anybody and not to be discouraged. She would catch up.

One day, someone called me a frog.

"That's what we call the Frenchies," Zoey said at lunch.

"It's a dumb insult," Peggy said. "Don't feel bad, Karin."

A few days later, I heard someone talk about being "Jewed down," and Peggy explained that meant getting cheated by someone cheap.

"That's what you think about me?" I asked.

"No, no! It's just an expression."

And then a few days later, two girls came up to me in the hall and said, "Dirty Jew."

I kept a blank face and kept going down the hall. I was surprised—shocked, really. I didn't think Americans were like that. I didn't tell anyone. I didn't even think I was that upset.

After supper, I sat down at the table in our room and worked on my homework. I had to memorize ten spelling words and learn five vocabulary words: *Mundane, mercenary, mammoth, formidable, frantic*. Vocabulary was harder than spelling. Then I read one chapter in my history book and, hardest of all, outlined a story called "The Red Barn" from my English book. The last thing I did was math homework. Last, because Marc had told me I should always do the hardest things first, then the easy ones.

I got ready for bed. I went down the hall to the bathroom to change into my pajamas and brush my teeth. Marc was still reading when I returned. I put my doll on the pillow near me. "Good night, Marc."

I closed my eyes and turned onto my favorite side, but I couldn't fall asleep. For a long, long time, I tossed around. And, then, I started thinking. I thought about Paris and my friend Sarah Olinski. I remembered how we had loved each other, how we planned our lives together, how we were always going to be best friends. And I wondered where she was now. Was she alive?

Then I thought about Papa, and I shouldn't have. My throat swelled. I buried my head in the pillow so Marc wouldn't hear me cry.

After all you've been through, to let any of these people at school bother you... It was Maman's voice. She was speaking to me. *Why be upset, even for a moment, over such stupidity? No, darling, do as well as you can; be honest, be loving, and the rest will take care of itself....*

25

PEGGY'S HOUSE

"OSWEGO IS LIKE Paris, I think," I said, as Peggy and I walked down Oak Street. It was after school, and I was going home with her.

"Paris! Paris is a big city, Karin. You're nuts."

"I mean, a little it's the same. Both have rivers within the city, and bridges also, and streets named for trees. Yes?"

"How neat!" Peggy said.

"Yes. How neat!"

She linked her arm through mine. "I'm glad you

came here, Karin. It's fun having you. I really, really like knowing you."

"I, also," I said, "like knowing you. Thank you."

"All you have to say when you agree is 'Me, too.'"

"'Me, too'?"

"Uh-huh. That means when I say I like you, you're saying the same back to me. It saves a lot of words. Get it?"

"Okay. Get it!"

Peggy lived on Ash Street in a little house painted light green. It had a square front porch and a garage, like a second tiny house at the end of the driveway. "Ma!" she yelled, when we went in. "I'm home. Ma, Karin is here. She's from the fort."

Her mother came down the stairs. "Karin? I've heard about you." She looked me over carefully. "How do you like it here, dear?"

I smoothed my hair. "I like it very much. Thank you. This is my first American house."

Mrs. Bradbury smiled. "Peggy can show you around."

She showed me the living room first. Lace doilies on the arms of the couch, framed pictures of Peggy and her sisters, overstuffed chairs. Then the kitchen with its big refrigerator and the cat, Maypo, sleeping on a chair. And upstairs, the bedroom she shared with her sister, Mary. Twin maple beds, blue chenille bedspreads, a maple bureau with a mirror, a shelf for Peggy's doll collection.

I smoothed out the white dress on a bride doll. All the dolls had shiny yellow curls, tiny noses, and little red mouths. "I had a doll. Name of Felice," I said. "And also the stuffed dog, Maurice."

And then we both shouted, "Maurice and Felice!"

"Okay, now we have to make a wish." Peggy linked her pinkie with mine. "Ready? What goes up a chimney?"

"Smoke?"

"Right. What comes down a chimney?"

"Down a chimney? Chimney boy to clean?"

"Santa Claus, Karin!"

"Oh. Okay."

"What goes through a needle? Come on, you know that one. Doesn't your mother sew?"

"It's the American word, I'm not sure. String?"

"No, thread."

"Oh yes. Thread."

"Now close your eyes and make a wish."

"Will it come true?"

"Of course."

I closed my eyes. There was only one wish.

"May your wish and mine come true," Peggy chanted. "Okay, you can open your eyes now."

"When does the wish come true?" I asked.

"Oh no. It's not serious. It's just, you know, super-stition. Do you like my room?"

"Yes, beautiful," I said. And I tried to remember my bedroom, the room I had shared with Grand-mère for eight years. I reminded myself that the bureau held Grand-mère's creams and lotions, that I'd had a white cupboard for my books and there were lacy curtains at the long windows. But they were only words, and the picture wouldn't come.

"Karin!" Peggy jiggled my arm. "What's up? You look like a zombie."

"A what?" I followed her up the stairs to the attic. Flies buzzed against the dusty windows. Boxes were piled in corners. "Someone could live up here," I said.

"Oh no. It's too hot. And look, you'd bump your head on the rafters. My dad keeps saying he'll make a playroom up here. Oh, sure—when I'm too old!"

I bent down and opened a small door built into the eaves. "What is this for?"

"Just someplace to put things away."

The space went way back on both sides, under the roof. "Someone could hide in here," I said.

"I know. Mary used to when she was little—get in there and hide, and everyone would be running around yelling for her. My mom told me."

"More than one person, even," I said.

You would have to squat or lie down, but there was

more room here than in the hole we'd dug in Monsieur Taubert's cellar. You could hardly tell the door was there. All you'd have to do was cover it with a trunk, and if they didn't pull the trunk away, you'd be safe from the soldiers.

But there were no soldiers here. Well, there were, but they were American soldiers. They smiled when we showed them our passes in the morning, and they said things like "You have fun today, kids."

In the kitchen, Peggy's mother was sitting at the table, smoking a cigarette and reading the newspaper. "Peggy giving you the tour, Karin?" she said.

"I'm showing her everything," Peggy said. "We're going to look at the backyard now."

She showed me their apple tree, which still had a few apples hanging on it. We walked farther, to the back of the yard. "This is where my mother has a garden in the summer. Did your mother have a garden?"

"No. We lived in an apartment."

"Poor you, living in a city where you can't even have a backyard or a garden."

"We had a terrace," I said. Then I wondered if that was true, but I kept talking. "A fig tree in a pot. Lots of plants and flowers in pots. Grand-mère took care of them."

"Who's Gremare?"

"No." I pronounced it for her again. "Grand-mère." I bent to pick up a gold-colored leaf. Bugs had chewed minuscule holes in it. "Mother's mother."

"Oh, your granny! Say *grandmother*."

"Grand-mère," I said again. I would never say "grandmother."

I held the leaf up to the sun, and as I did, I remembered a dream I'd had about Grand-mère. She'd been on the terrace, wearing a gold skirt, bending over to water the flowers. It was like the dream about me and Maman in the park. I saw everything clearly, even the light in her hair. Wasn't it strange that when I tried to remember something, I couldn't, but in my dreams, I remembered perfectly.

26

SHAKING STARS

I WAS ALONE in the room. Marc had gone out without telling me where. He only said he'd be back soon. Sometimes I liked being alone, but that night the silence seemed big.

Where had he gone that he couldn't ask me to come with him?

I turned on the radio, then turned it off. What if he didn't come back? A stupid thought. "But what if he doesn't?" I said out loud.

I stood at the window. I wouldn't die if I were alone here. I knew how to take care of myself. And when the war ended, I'd go back to Maman. The same thought, the one I thought every day. I'd go to Valence. I'd find Maman. Then we'd go back to Paris, rue Erlanger, our home.

I loved this thought.

But without Marc? Impossible.

But what if he was standing on the side of a road right now, his thumb up, looking for a ride? Where? I knew the answer to that: *anywhere.* Anywhere else. He kept talking about going places. Being free. Freedom.

Days after he'd done it, he told me that he, Tomas, and some other boys had sneaked under the fence and hitchhiked to Syracuse. "We didn't want to come back in three hours! We wanted to come back when we were ready."

They bought hamburgers, strolled around the city, went up to the college and "goofed around." He'd kept it a secret from me. Were there other secrets? Maybe what he meant by "free" was free of me, the responsibility of me. Free of being with me when he wanted to be with his friends.

I checked the clock and sat down to do homework, then jumped up and checked it again. A baby was crying somewhere. I resisted the feeling of wanting to cry, too.

I put on a sweater and went out. The night was cool, dark, and starry. I walked across the parade ground and up the hill to the old fort. The lake was silvery black. I lay down on the ground and looked up. Mrs. Stein had taught me to recognize the constellation Cassiopeia, which looked like a necklace. It was a cold night, and the stars were shaking.

The wind blew through the grass and I thought of where I was on this hill, near the lake of an American town. The stars were so vast, they covered me, and they covered the lake and the whole United States, and Italy and France and Maman. I lay there, staring up, until the stars blurred in my eyes.

When I got back to the room, Marc was there on the cot, smoking his before-bed cigarette. He had taken up smoking recently, and he loved it. He smoked one cigarette in the morning and one just before he went to sleep. He would lie with one hand behind his head, holding his cigarette between his thumb and forefinger in the other hand, exactly as Papa used to. Tomas smoked, too. They bought their cigarettes together, two at a time in town, at the cigar store.

"Where were you?" Marc pointed to the clock with his cigarette. "Why were you out so late?"

I took off my sneakers and socks. "I went for a walk."

"You should have left me a note." He blew smoke out from the corner of his mouth. I hated the way he did that, as if he were twenty-four instead of fourteen.

"You go out, Marc. You don't tell me where you're going. So I can go out, too. And I don't have to tell you. Why should I? Where were you?"

"Never mind that. I'm responsible for you. I'm older than you. I can do things you can't."

I threw my sneakers on the floor. "Yes. I'm sure Maman would love that you went out without even telling me where."

He stubbed out his cigarette on the floor. "Don't always be bringing Maman into it. She has nothing to do with my life."

"Nothing to do with it?" The breath went out of me, as if he'd punched me. "That's a lie. You're a liar, Marc! She has everything to do with you, your life, my life, everything, every—every—" I hardly knew what I was saying. I touched my chest. "Maman's here, right here in me, with me, and—"

"Don't get upset," Marc interrupted. "I'm only saying, do you see Maman? No. Who do you see? Who's here? Me. That's what you see. That's who's here. Not Maman. So that's what I meant. It's not a lie, just the truth."

"Take it back, Marc! Tell me where you went and take that back, or I'll never speak to you again."

"I'm *so* frightened," he said. He got up and draped a blanket over the line he'd hung between our cots for privacy.

I got into bed and pulled the sheet up to my chin. I was still wearing my clothes. "Go to hell," I said. "Go to hell! You're not my brother anymore!"

Dearest Maman,

Marc and I had a big fight. I was angry and I swore at him, and now we're not speaking. For two days we haven't talked unless we absolutely had to. I don't think the fight was just my fault, Maman. I don't want to fight with my brother, and I know you wouldn't want me to, but sometimes it seems that I can't help myself. Well, I don't feel so much like writing now. I love you, Maman. I'll try to be a better person, the way you would want me to be.

Your Karin

Dearest Maman,

Last week, Marc asked me if I wanted to stay out of school to show respect for the holidays of Rosh Hashanah and Yom Kippur. He said he was going to do that. I said I would also. Then he said we might as well go to the services, even though we're not a religious family. And I said I thought that was a good idea, although really, Maman, I hadn't thought about it at all. Marc said he remembered us going to temple with Grand-mère in Paris on the High Holy Days. I don't remember that. I wish I did.

Maman, what I liked most about Rosh Hashanah was how happy everyone was because it was the beginning of the new year. "Everything starts fresh now," Mr. Stein said. All the people were happy to see us. They were shaking hands and wishing one another a happy and good and safe new year.

Another thing I liked was when the rabbi blew the shofar at Yom Kippur services. It gave me chills. And I thought how, for two thousand years, Jews have heard the shofar on this day and been reminded to live a good life. That's what the rabbi said in his sermon.

And then he said we should go to anyone we had hurt and apologize, so we could begin the new year with a clean heart.

It was as if he was talking to me, Maman. I turned to Marc to say I was sorry for our fight and anything mean I had said. And at the very same moment, he turned to me. We said "sorry" to each other, and I said, "I really mean it," and we hugged and sort of cried. And now that we've made up, Maman, _everything_ seems better. Even the weather! The maple and elm trees are all golden and red. One really big tree I see on the way to school every day shines like copper. The boats go up and down the lake, and the wind blows, and everyone says winter is coming, but it's hard to believe because the sun shines so beautifully!

Good night, Maman. I love you.

Your Karin

27

AN AMERICAN
FAMILY

PEGGY'S MOTHER invited Marc and me to eat Thanksgiving dinner with their family, but Marc already had another invitation from one of his school friends. Almost all the children and a lot of the adults from the fort were invited to Thanksgiving dinners in town.

"Karin, I hear much good food comes in this holiday," Eva said. We walked part of the way from the fort to our friends' houses together. "Eat big," she advised me when we parted.

Peggy was waiting for me at the door. The house was noisy with people. Her parents, four cousins, an aunt and uncle, her sister Mary, Mary's boyfriend, Kevin, and her sister Jane were all in the living room. Peggy introduced me to everybody, saying one name after another. I kept smiling and saying, "Pleased to meet you." The only person I already knew besides Peggy's mother was her sister Jane. Peggy always called her "Jane the Glamour-puss."

After another cousin arrived, we went into the dining room. Peggy sat me between herself and her uncle James, or was it Jim? I thought I'd heard him called by both names.

The table was loaded with delicious food. There was a huge turkey with "stuffing," plus all sorts of vegetables. "Glazed carrots," Peggy said, pointing. "Fried potatoes, baked sweet potatoes, squash with honey, green beans, beets—"

"Just no cabbage," I said. "Okeydokey?"

Her uncle laughed. "Don't like cabbage, huh, honey? I'm with you on that."

"Well, I'm thankful for this holiday," Peggy's aunt Myra said. She stood up and rapped on a glass with a fork. "Grace," she said.

I looked around. I thought she was calling someone. They all bowed their heads.

"Thank you, Lord, for this bountiful meal," Peggy's

aunt said. "Thank you for keeping us safe. Thank you for everything good in our lives. Thank you for letting us share our meal with Peggy's new friend."

Peggy poked me and glanced at me with a little smile. "You," she mouthed.

"Amen," Peggy's uncle said. And then everyone said, "Amen." Everyone except me. It was like not saying the Pledge of Allegiance. Not to be disrespectful to Peggy's family, but it wasn't my prayer.

"Okay, folks, let's go." Peggy's father stood up, reached for a knife, and started carving the turkey. They passed around the platters of food. I thought the cranberry sauce was Jell-O.

"No, no. Just try it," Peggy said. I did, and I liked it much more than Jell-O.

Peggy's father told me to eat until I was "too full."

"Until you're stuffed," Peggy's aunt Myra said. "That's how we celebrate our holiday." She had blond hair like Peggy and the same little nose. "We eat like pigs."

"Speak for yourself, lady," Peggy's father said.

They all started telling stories about how much they'd eaten on other Thanksgiving holidays.

Later, when the pies and ice cream came out, Peggy's uncle asked me about the war. Every time he asked a question, everyone would stop talking and look at me.

"So was it awful over there, young lady?" he said.

"Yes, yes. It was."

"And you and your brother—Peggy says you're all alone over here?"

"Well, we are with the other people in the fort."

"Now, how did your parents let you come here all alone?"

"How—" I started to stutter. "My—my—mother, you see—"

"Her mother was too sick to come," Peggy put in. I had told her a little, but not everything.

"Your mother was sick, young lady?"

"Yes."

"Very sick, I take it, if she couldn't travel with you?"

"Yes."

Most of his questions I answered like that, just yes or no. I didn't know what else to say. What could I say when he asked if Marc and I had escaped from the Nazis? Yes, but it wasn't something that happened in a single moment or a single day or even a single month.

To tell it, where would I start? With the yellow stars we had to wear? With being put out of school? Or would it be with Papa's arrest? And if I told that much, then I'd have to go on, about Madame Zetain, and Monsieur Taubert, and all the rest of it.

I smiled when they looked at me. I liked being

there with Peggy's family, and I could tell that her mother, especially, was happy to have me there. I didn't want to have any sad thoughts. Just once, though, I thought, *We Levis aren't a big family—not anymore.* And for a little while, I was quiet.

28

REPORT CARDS

IN SCHOOL one day, Mr. Anderson, the history teacher, pulled down the map of the world and pointed to where American soldiers were fighting. Zoey Hendlin raised her hand. "Mr. Anderson, do we have to talk about the war all the time?" She looked at me, as if I was the only one who would be interested.

But when Mr. Anderson asked who had grown a victory garden the summer before, almost everyone in class raised their hands. Peggy said her family saved bacon grease and silver foil from her dad's cigarette packs to help the war effort. "Who has a relative in the military?" Mr. Anderson asked. More people raised their hands, and Royal Sutter, who sat in back and never said a word, said his father was missing in action.

Later, Peggy passed me a note. "My so-called friend, Zoey, is so-called jealous of so-called you!" It was Peggy's latest thing, to say "so-called" about everything. She whispered, "Answer!"

"She should not be," I wrote, and passed the note back.

Mr. Anderson didn't even notice, but for the rest of the class, I felt sort of sick. I always felt that way when I broke rules, even the little ones about not chewing gum in school and not speaking without raising your hand first. I would think, *What if I'm caught? What if I'm sent to the principal's office? What if I'm sent back to the fort? Disgraced?*

"You wouldn't be disgraced," Peggy said.

"And what if you were sent to the principal? So what?" Zoey said. We were sitting together at lunch. "If it was me, my father would have kittens, but you don't have anybody who cares. Lucky you, you can do what you want."

"So-called lucky me," I said. I made it a joke. But again I felt a little sick. Nobody who cared? What about Marc? And the Steins? And Maman? Maman, most of all. She cared, she would always care, even if she wasn't with me. Should I say it? Make Zoey listen to me and understand?

No. I decided not to, as usual. People said things to me, and maybe they upset me, but I kept quiet.

"Did you hear that Richie Russell's father was arrested?" Zoey said to Peggy.

"Richie's father! What for?"

"Fraud." Zoey licked peanut butter from her fingers. "My mom heard it on the radio. Did you see Richie? He came to school, like nothing happened. I would die if it was me and my father was arrested."

"Maybe he came to school," I said, "because his father didn't do anything wrong."

"Why would they arrest him then?" Zoey looked at me as if I were stupid.

"A person could be arrested for not anything," I said.

"Oh no, they couldn't! People are arrested because they're criminals. And if your father was arrested, you would want to die of disgrace. *That's* disgrace," she said.

"Die?" I said. "No. Here I am, still living."

Zoey and Peggy both stared.

"You mean your father was arrested?" Peggy said at last.

"Yes."

"*Why?*"

"Because he is Jewish."

"Just because of that?" Zoey looked at Peggy. "I mean, I know they made our Lord suffer, but just because you're Jewish doesn't seem like a reason to go to jail."

I was sorry I had said anything. I took a drink of milk. The coldness went up into my forehead and made it throb. Better to think of that than of Papa and how they took him away.

Every day, it seemed, there was something else that bothered me—not always big things, sometimes just little things, like making a mess of my spelling paper or forgetting lunch money. I told myself I should be more careful. I should be better. I should not let myself be upset. Why wasn't I more like Marc?

Everything seemed easier for him. He did better in school than I did. He studied more, but I didn't think that was the big difference. The language *was* still much easier for him, but it was more than that. He just knew he was going to do better than me; he always did. Besides, he said Maman had already taught him everything he was supposed to be learning now.

On my first report card, I had Cs and Bs. "That's good," Marc said, but how good could it be when he got all As? We had to have an adult sign our report cards. Marc asked Mr. Stein. I didn't want the Steins to compare me to Marc, so I wanted to ask Jo to sign mine, but she was in the hospital, having her baby.

"I have no one to sign my report card," I said.

"Mr. Stein will sign it," Marc said. "Or Mrs. Stein."

"She'll think I'm dumb."

"Relax," Marc said. "Cs and Bs? That's A-OK. Take it easy."

His newest American expressions. "Relax." "A-OK." "Take it easy." He whistled a lot, too. *Why is he so happy?* That was a mean thing to think, but I thought it anyway.

Since Thanksgiving, the weather had been getting colder. It had snowed almost every day, and our room was chilly. The morning I had to return my report card, I woke up grouchy. Marc was whistling. "Do you have to be so noisy?" I said.

He looked over at me and laughed. "Take it easy," he said, and he went back to whistling.

One Saturday, Peggy brought her sled to the fort, and she and I and Marika went sledding on the hill that sloped down to the lake—the same place where Marika and Trudi and I had gone swimming only a few months before.

Later, we went downtown to look in the shop windows. We were walking on Bridge Street when Marika said, "Your brother, Karin. Across the street."

He was with a girl who was wearing a big white ski sweater and a white headband on her red hair. "Oh, I know her," Peggy said. "That's Barbara Henderson. She's in high school."

"Your brother has a girlfriend!" Marika said.

"Not him," I said. "He's too shy. She must be just a friend."

But I knew Marika was right. I could tell from the way Marc was walking with the girl—so close—that she was more than a friend. And I knew that was his secret, where he'd gone that night, why he whistled in the morning.

At first, I thought I'd tell him that I knew his secret, I knew about his girlfriend. I even knew her name. I imagined his surprise. His cigarette would fall right out of his mouth.

But then, I decided no, I wouldn't say anything. I'd wait for him to tell me. Yes, I wanted to do it that way. I wanted him to tell me.

29

MARC'S
LITTLE SECRET

MARC KEPT LOOKING at his clock. We
were sitting at the table, studying. Every few minutes,
he'd glance up and turn the clock toward him. Exactly
at eight, he jumped up. "I have to go out for a while."
He combed his hair, smoothing it back.

"Where are you going?"

"Just out."

"Out where? What're you going to do?"

"Nothing much. Get those X-ray eyes off me." He
put on his jacket and wound a scarf around his neck.

"Marc, tell me where you're going."

"Don't be a pest, Karin. I'll be back in a while, all right?"

"No, not 'all right.' It's too cold to go out." That was absurd. It *was* cold—the temperature had dropped below twenty degrees—but we still went out all the time. "And it's dark," I said. Another silly remark.

He gave me a tap on the head. "I won't be gone long. Finish your homework. You can visit someone if you get bored." And he was out the door.

"Okay," I said to the empty room. "Hunky-dory. Fine with me." I knew how to be alone. I had plenty to do. Besides homework, I had started drawing again. The art teacher, Mr. Milleritz, said I should work at it. He was helping me.

I put Betty Lou next to the clock on the table, and then I added a jar. Mr. Milleritz said I should practice drawing objects for a while. I started drawing, but my fingers slipped on the pencil, and my eyes suddenly filled with tears.

I wished I could see Marc, not even to talk to him but just to know where he was and what he was doing. *What if he's meeting the red-haired girl? Why does it matter—it doesn't! Stop waiting for him to say something about her—tell him you know his secret.*

I stood at the window, scraping the frosted pane with my fingernail. Maybe they were talking about me, about what a pest I was. How Marc could never be free with me here. Marika thought I was too possessive of Marc, but I never kept him from doing anything. It would only be courteous for him to tell me where he was going! Anyway, Marika didn't know how it felt to be alone. She had her mother and an older sister, and they never went anywhere without her.

About an hour later, I heard Marc stamping his feet in the hall. "Cold outside!" he said, coming in. His cheeks were bright red. "My hands are freezing."

"Lucky me, staying in," I said.

He acted as if he didn't get my sarcasm. He grinned. "You're smart. What'd you do? Were you drawing?"

I sat down on the cot. I told myself not to be possessive, not to say anything about the red-haired girl. And then I said it anyway. "Marc, I know your secret."

"What secret? I don't have any secrets." He pulled a cigarette from his pocket and lit it.

"I saw you with a girl last week. Red hair and fat arms. You were on Bridge Street, right across the street from me and Marika and Peggy. You didn't even notice us."

He exhaled smoke.

"You're stinking up the room, Marc! Is that where you were just now? With that redheaded girl? I know her name, too. Barbara. Did you go see Barbara that other time?"

"What other time?"

"When we had the fight. When you wouldn't tell me anything. And then we made up, but you're still the same, you're still not telling me anything." My face was burning. I thought I was going to cry. No, no, no! I pulled my pad in front of me and started drawing on it, nothing really, just squiggly lines to keep myself busy.

"Oh, you might as well know." Marc puffed on his cigarette, narrowing his eyes, as if he were older than God. He wasn't the same boy I'd walked with through Italy. "I just went out to phone her."

"You were talking on the phone all this time?"

He nodded. He looked pleased with himself. "And Barbara doesn't have fat arms, Karin. She's in eleventh grade," he added, too casually.

"Eleventh grade! How old is she?"

"Seventeen."

"Marc! You're only fourteen."

"Almost fifteen," he said. "Three more months. Anyway, she doesn't care."

"What do you talk about?"

"None of your business, actually."

"I thought you liked Eva."

"I do. Eva is a very smart girl. We have fantastic discussions."

"Then why do you have to run to this so-called Barbara?"

"She's very nice, very sympathetic. She says I'm more mature than American boys. More serious. She doesn't want me to smoke. See, she's a good influence. We met in the history club."

"What does so-called dumb Barbara see in you?"

"She's not dumb, and what is this 'so-called' stuff, anyway?"

"Just something Peggy and I say. Do you neck with her?"

"Neck?" He got a faintly goofy look in his eyes. "What's that?"

"You *know* what that is." I made smacking sounds.

"It's not a question you can ask, Karin."

"I can ask you anything I want."

"But I don't have to answer." He stubbed out his cigarette in a little tin ashtray.

"Maaarc." I sat down on the edge of my cot. "You shouldn't."

"What, have a girlfriend? It's natural."

"You're too young!" I felt stupid saying that, and, at the same time, stubborn. I kept thinking of him with her, looking at her so eagerly, talking, talking, not even noticing me right across the street. And meeting her in secret, running out to phone her in secret, not telling me anything. Was he telling her things instead?

"Maman wouldn't like it," I said. "She wouldn't approve."

He stared at me, then he flung himself down on his bed. I thought he would argue with me. But he didn't say anything, just lay there on his back, his chin raised, almost as if he'd been thinking the same thing.

30

THE SODA SHOP

MARIKA, TRUDI, Peggy, and I walked around Oswego together, looking at the Christmas decorations on the houses. Trudi was happy again. She'd been miserable when she was put back into the third grade, but it got better after a while. The little kids helped her, and they didn't laugh at her accent or because she was bigger. In a month, she had moved up a grade, and the next month, another grade.

Around us was a white world. The whole town of Oswego, houses and trees, glittered and sparkled. It was winter vacation, and it had been snowing for three days. Big, soft, light snowflakes falling, falling, falling. Walls of snow taller than we were had grown up between the sidewalks and the roads. Cars passed, nearly invisible, their tire chains thumping.

On Elm Street, four boys on skis glided past us, right in the middle of the street.

"Hi! How are you?" they called.

"Hello!" we said. "Hello! Hi!"

"Enough snow for you girls?"

"Mucho plenty," Peggy sang out.

"Mucho plenty," we all sang out.

And then we kept walking and talking.

"There she is," Marc said. He walked a little faster. Barbara was waiting in front of the soda shop for us. She was wearing ski pants and the same big white sweater and a white headband.

"Hi, Karin!" She waved as if she knew me already. "I'm so glad I'm getting to meet you."

Her deep voice surprised me. "Hello," I said. I dug my hands into my jacket pockets and followed her and Marc into the warm, steamy soda shop. There was a row of dark, high-backed booths. For a moment, Marc looked from me to Barbara, then sat down next to me. I didn't think I should feel as glad as I did—but I did.

The waitress came, and Barbara ordered a lemon

Coke. I ordered fries and Marc ordered a cheeseburger. He loved cheeseburgers more than any other American food.

Then none of us said anything for a while.

"You know what, Karin?" Barbara said. "I always wanted a sister. Somebody to talk things over with. I'm an only child. I don't have any brothers or sisters."

"Oh," I said. I wondered why she was telling me this.

"I'm like her brother now," Marc said.

"Yeah, he's my new brother," Barbara said.

"Little brother," I said. "He's fourteen."

"I know." Her face got a little flushed.

"Fifteen soon," Marc said. "Two more months, that's not too long."

"Three months," I said. "March."

Marc smiled. "Fine. Three months." He leaned on his hand, looking at Barbara. Straight at her chest.

"Maaarc," I said.

"What?"

"Nothing." I glared at him.

"You two have a wonderful relationship," Barbara said. "Marc talks about you all the time, Karin. I hear you're very smart, too. Marc is so smart! He puts me to shame."

"Oh," I said doubtfully. "You like to study?"

"Karin," Marc said, with a warning in his voice.

"I do," Barbara said. "I'm an A student. I'm in the National Honor Society." She looked at me with a smile. "Surprised?"

"Oh no," I lied.

She brought her white hair band down, then pushed it back on her head. "You know, Karin, Marc says you're not so happy that we're, you know, friends."

Why had Marc told her that? What else had he told her? The things I'd said about her? "Fat arms"... "this so-called Barbara"... "dumb"... I folded a straw into a tiny accordion. I thought, as I had before, that if Maman were here, I would be a nicer person. Better. I wouldn't have so many mean thoughts.

"So I was thinking, we—you and I—maybe we could be friends, too. Really. I would like it if you could be sort of like my younger sister."

Her younger sister? No. I was Marc's younger sister. Marc's, not Barbara's!

"My mother died when I was seven years old. She had leukemia. She died so fast. I mean, she went to the hospital, and she was gone."

For an instant I wondered if she'd made that up to make me feel sorry for her, but her eyes were watery. "I'm sorry," I said.

She raised her shoulders. "I just wanted you to know that, you know, that I understand about you and Marc and, um, you know, all the things that you two—"

"See what kind of person she is, Karin?" Marc said.

He was looking at Barbara as if she was so special. I kept folding the straw, tinier and tinier.

I knew I should say something bigger and warmer than "I'm sorry" or "I understand." She'd lost someone she loved, too. I put the folded straw into my pocket. I didn't say anything. I couldn't, not with the way Marc was looking at her, as if he really loved her. Loved Barbara, not me.

Dearest Maman,

Today is Monday, January 1, the first day of 1945. We have now been in America nearly five months. It seems a very long time and very far away from you.

Last night, everyone stayed up until midnight. We had a big party in the recreation room. The camp director, Mr. Joseph Smart, was there. Everyone from the fort was there, too, all the children, all the adults. We all acted happy and silly, and we all shouted "Happy New Year!" when it was midnight. I did the same as everyone, but in my heart, Maman, it was different. It was quiet. Is this the year we will be together again? I pray for it.

Maman, here is the worst thing about being away from you—there's nothing I can do to bring me back to you. There's nothing I can do to make it happen sooner or faster. There's nothing I can do to change anything. All I can do is wait. And sometimes, Maman, that's very, very hard. I love you.

Your Karin

31

"THANKS, AMERICAN BOY"

IN FEBRUARY, the wind blew all the time, an icy wind off the lake, a cold breath that never stopped. It penetrated windows and doors and walls, and blew right into our bones. And then, just when it seemed as if the world was always going to be frozen, March came and the weather warmed up.

As I left school one day, Royal Sutter caught up with me. "You're one of the fort people," he said, as if it had just occurred to him. His eyebrows were so pale they were almost silver. "You still living there?" he asked.

"Oh yes."

"So you're a Jewish person?"

I wanted to laugh. It was the way he said it—"a Jewish person," curious but not mean—and the fact that he was asking me these questions after all the months that we'd been in the same classes together.

"Do you like it here?" he asked.

Another question so old it was like stale bread! "Yes," I said. "I do like it here."

"How about the weather?"

"What about it?"

"Do you like it?" he asked.

"Now—dripping—it's nicer," I said. "It's too cold in February."

"Hot dog!" he said.

"'Hot dog'?"

"That means 'You said it!' We get some snow, don't we? I mean we get *snow*." He raised his hand above his head to show the size of the snowdrifts. "You ever see snow like that where you come from?"

"No," I said.

"I didn't think so. One winter we were snowed in. Oh, man. The snow fell and fell. We couldn't get out of our house. Not out the door. We got out the second-story window. We made a slide from the window to the ground, and down we went. You should have seen my old grandpa sliding on his rear end out that window."

"Is that true?" I asked.

"True blue." He put his hand on his heart. "Your name is Karin, right?"

"Yes."

"So, are you going to live here? I mean, live here all the time, after the war?"

I shook my head. "We have to go back to our own country."

"What for?"

"I want to go back," I said. "And your government says we must."

"Oh, the government," he said. "My old grandpa says don't trust the government."

"Your government is good. It brought us here. Your President Roosevelt and your government."

"Maybe you could stay," he said. "You could write letters and tell them you want to stay."

"Some people, yes," I said. "Not me."

He stared at me with his pale blue eyes under the silver eyebrows. "You know what, Karin? You're cute."

"Me? I am? Thank you."

"Yeah, you're welcome." Suddenly, he walked off. Then he turned and said, "I like talking to you."

"Okay," I said. "Thanks, American boy. Me, too."

"'American boy'?" he said. "You are very cute!"

Dearest Maman,

Mr. Franklin Delano Roosevelt, the American president, is dead. Did you hear about it? The newspapers say that all over the world people are crying. All the Americans we know are tremendously sad. My girlfriend Peggy said her parents cried. Here, at the fort, everyone was crying. He was a great man. Mr. Stein and some of the other men said the prayer for the dead for him.

But, Maman, that's not the only news. Today, Monday, April 30, only a little more than two weeks after Mr. Roosevelt died, we heard the news that Adolf Hitler is dead. Marc and I heard it on the radio. We couldn't even speak at first. Then we hugged each other. Maman, he was so evil, it can't be wrong to be happy that he's dead.

Mr. Stein says this has to mean the war will come to an end soon. Dearest Maman, I think of only one thing. We'll be together. Soon, soon.

Your Karin

32

SOMETHING BAD

THE MOMENT Marc came into the room, I knew he'd been with Barbara. It was something about the way he walked, strutted almost. "You were with her, weren't you?" I said. "Barbara."

"So?"

"So...nothing." Now that I'd said it, what else was there to say? I bent my head and opened my book. I was reading *Daddy-Long-Legs* for the third time. This time I could read most of it.

"What did you do?" I asked.

"Oh, we walked around and talked."

"What else?"

"Nothing." Marc hung his jacket on a peg.

"Just talked? I don't believe you."

"Karin. Believe me. We talked. We talk a lot. She's a serious girl. She likes to talk to me."

"And kiss?" I said.

"All right, that's too much," he said. "Now stop."

"Why her?" I said. "If you want a girlfriend, choose Eva. She's beautiful, smart, and she's like us. She came with us on the ship. How can you forget that? Barbara's not even Jewish."

"Eva's not Jewish, either. I never thought I'd hear you saying something like that. What difference does it make, Jewish or not? Barbara's a person."

"Maybe she's not Jewish, but you know what I mean. I'm sorry that she lost her mother, but it's not... not the same." My eyes were sticky and hot. I thought of Maman, of Mr. Stein and Mrs. Stein, of Jo and Eva. And I seemed to see them all pointing at me. *Shame on you... shame on you...*

After we shut off the lights, I couldn't sleep. I turned from one side to the other. I heard the clock ticking, the snow dripping as it melted, and the wind blowing around the building.

"Marc," I said into the darkness.

"What?"

"Are you sleeping?"

"Not yet."

"Are you mad at me?"

"No."

"Are you sure?"

"Yes. What is it, Karin?"

"I'm sorry I'm so mean about your girlfriend." I wrapped my blanket around me. There was a little light coming in from outside. I went over to his cot and sat down on the edge. "I'll try to be a better sister."

"You're a good sister."

"Do you mean it? You don't hate me?"

"No, I don't hate you." He sat up. "Why would you say that? Do you think I hate you, Karin? That is so crazy. You're my sister."

"I want to be better, but I miss Maman so much… I don't want to be mean. I know sometimes you wish you had another sister. You do, don't you? You can say it."

"Never, I never wished that. I never wanted any sister but you."

"Marc." I wiped my eyes on my pajamas sleeve. "I just don't want you to leave me. If you left me, I don't know… I don't think I could—"

"Leave you? Where did you get that idea? Who said anything about leaving you?"

"You know that Maman said we should stay together."

"And we will," he said. "We'll stay together. We have to. It's just us now."

"What do you mean?" I pulled the blanket tighter around me. "Don't say that!"

"I'm tired, Karin. Let's both go back to sleep."

"Wait, wait. No, it's not just us! Why did you say that, 'just us'? Just us? What about Maman?"

"I don't know. Leave me alone." He rubbed his eyes. "We'll talk about Maman in the morning."

I went to the window and looked out, but I couldn't focus, I couldn't see anything. *Something is happening. Something is happening here, right now, in this room. Something bad.*

"Marc." I said his name again. "Marc." Everything was wavering, blurry, as if I were underwater. "Marc. Tell me."

There was silence, then he said, "Maman—"

"What? What about Maman?"

"She..."

"She's dead?" I said. I sat down on the floor. "Maman's dead?"

He nodded.

"How do you know?"

"I know."

Calm covered me like a blanket. Through it, I

heard myself saying words—"For how long? You've known for how long?"—but they weren't my words, they were like objects that seemed to hang in the air. I said the words, I heard the words, but nothing touched me, nothing reached me. I was only conscious of how steady my voice was…and the words, the ordinary words.

33

THE DARKNESS OF SLEEP

I LAY IN BED with my eyes open. It hurt to breathe. I lay there listening to night sounds. The creaking of the wooden floors. The wind against the windows. Marc's breathing.

What if he was wrong? Maybe he was miserable and wanted someone else to be miserable, too. For a moment, I believed it.

Maman . . . Maman, Maman, Maman . . .

The darkness of sleep came toward me, big and soft.

In the morning, when Marc got out of bed, he looked at me. He didn't say anything. He opened the window and leaned into the air. Wind blew into the room. Not a big cold March wind, not a soft April wind. It was a May wind, sweet, like leaves. Maman loved that smell.

Marc came and sat on the edge of my cot. "Hello," he said. Then for a while he didn't say anything.

"It's true?" I said.

He nodded.

"You knew on the boat, didn't you?" I said.

"Yes."

"That man from Valence?"

"Yes. You asked me if he knew anything about Monsieur Taubert, and I said he didn't." He paused. "He had heard about Monsieur, the people he took in. Saved. He knew about the children who had left, too, and the…the mother who died." He looked tired. "I wanted to tell you, Karin, but I couldn't. I tried. I lost my nerve every time."

"I don't want it to be true."

"I know," he said.

"Marc, I don't want it to be true!" I butted my head against his shoulder, and he held me, and I cried.

Dearest Maman,

This letter will go with the others I've written you. Now I know that you'll never see these letters. There's no point in going on with writing you, is there, but who else can I write to? Who else can I tell everything? Who else—

34

A CHANT,
A PRAYER

THERE WERE things I had to think about, things I needed to understand. Like about the letters I'd written to Maman: I wrote them so she could read them. That's why anyone writes a letter. So someone else will read it. I still had the letters, but no one to read them.

And I had to try to understand why Papa and Maman were gone. Why other people had parents and I didn't. Of course, I *understood*. The war...the war was the cause. But then why had there been a war? Oh yes. Hitler. The Germans. How they wanted other people's land. How they hated the Jews. I understood.

Yet, I didn't. I didn't understand anything. Only that I didn't have Papa or Maman anymore.

I stayed out of school for four days, then Marc said I should go back. He said Maman would want me to. So I did.

People spoke to me and maybe I answered. I really had no idea if I did or if I didn't. Somehow, the hours passed. The hours in school. The hours at the fort. A day began and a day ended, and with the end of the day, I could go to sleep.

I slept and slept, and every hour I slept felt like betrayal. All those hours when I wasn't thinking about Maman.

Marc talked to me. He was kind—kinder than he'd ever been. He kept trying to explain why he hadn't told me sooner. "Partly, I was protecting you. Partly, maybe, I was protecting myself. Because I knew the truth, but I never *really* knew it—didn't let myself know it until I told you."

He sat at night and read to me and talked to me. He said, and sometimes it sounded like a chant or a prayer, "We have each other. Karin, that hasn't changed. We have each other. That will never change."

35

BLUE SKIES

THE WAR in Europe ended early in May, when the Germans surrendered to the Allies. It was a day of blue skies. Everyone was out of the barracks, celebrating. A strange woman embraced me. "Remember this day. There'll never be another like it in our lives."

I moved from group to group, person to person. This was the day we had been waiting for. The war was over. We were free now. *Where are you, Maman?*

Later, I went into the woods. There was still snow here and there, in crevices and shadowed places. I made a little shrine with a handful of rounded, pink-streaked lake stones. I knelt and prayed for Maman, Papa, and Grand-mère. And for us, too, for Marc and me.

Maman was gone. And Papa was gone. They would never come back. And nothing could change that. "Patience," Papa used to say. "In time grass turns to milk." I was such a little girl then. I thought it was a miracle. Like a headline God made: GRASS TURNS TO MILK! But even if I could make miracles—drink the water in the ocean, count every grain of sand in the desert, pull the clouds from the sky—still Maman and Papa wouldn't come back.

I held one of the pink stones in the palm of my hand. It was smooth and round, and fit perfectly. I thought about all the places Marc and I had been, and all the things that had happened to us. I thought about everything I had learned. I had learned about hunger and pain. I had learned about people—some bad, some good. And I had learned that you can't look back for too long. You just have to keep going.

Dearest Maman,

My head and my heart are full of things to tell you. This will be the last letter I write you from Fort Ontario. First, I want to report that I did well on my exams and am now in eighth grade. Marc, of course, did wonderfully on his exams, all ninety-nines and one hundreds, and now he's in tenth grade. But, Maman, from now on, the year of 1946, we won't be going to school in Oswego.

All of us fort people can stay in America after all. The president and Congress have decided that if we want to, we can! Marc and I are going to live with Aunt Hannah in Del Rey, California. She's already sent us the train tickets.

Maman, you know she's not young, and my friend Jo says this can't be easy for her; but Aunt Hannah wants us and she is full of love for us. I know how lucky we are. So many people have been good to us. I've been thinking about that a lot, about how much we owe to people along the way.

I could start way back with Alena, remember her? She worked with Papa, and she was the one who found and brought us to Madame Zetain's. And Madame Zetain, of course, and the farmer and his wife who gave us food and let us sleep in the barn. Darling Monsieur Taubert. Maria Theresa. And then the American soldiers on the boat, and Mr. and Mrs. Stein, and Jo, and all my friends—Marika, Eva, Trudi, and Peggy. And Peggy's family, too! And so many other people.

Some people believe in Lady Luck (that's what the Americans call it) and some people believe in God. I believe in both, and also in the people who helped us along the way.

One more thing before I close this letter, Maman. Last night, I was half awake, or maybe half asleep, and I had a wonderful dream about our family. It was so familiar to me, Maman, so <u>true,</u> and yet I knew it was in my mind. Still, it seemed to me as if I were <u>inside</u> this dream—or story—whatever it was—as if it were really happening.

I'm going to write it down, so I never forget it. From now on, I intend to write down all my dreams. Maybe, someday, <u>my</u> daughter will read my dream book…yes, and my letters to you.

Maman, wherever you are, I believe that you know about the letters. And wherever you are, I believe you are here, with me. I know this as I know I will always love you.

Good night, Maman. Good night....

My Dream

I was walking down a long sandy road. There were tall trees on both sides, the sky was big and blue like the sea, and Maman was close behind me. I turned to see her. I looked at her for a long time. I was so happy that she was here, so happy. I was dancing on the road, and she smiled and called out, "Yes, darling. Yes!" Then Papa was there, too, and Marc and Grand-mère. We were together again. They were all here, all my beloveds, watching as I danced down the road under the blue, blue sky.

HISTORICAL NOTE

KARIN LEVI is a fictional character, yet her experiences in this novel are true to those of some Jews during World War II. The bitter truth is that six million people were murdered. Those who survived did so through a rare combination of chance and luck.

The anti-Jewish terror in Paris began on June 14, 1940, when the German army arrived and Julien Weill, the Grand Rabbi of Paris, was imprisoned. Between 1940 and 1944, Jewish-owned businesses were seized and given to non-Jews. Music by Jewish composers was prohibited. In the Louvre, the national gallery of art in Paris, all paintings with Jewish subjects were burned. The Café Dupont in Paris and other places of business posted notices: CLOSED TO DOGS AND JEWS. Telephones in Jewish homes were disconnected. Jews were permitted to shop only during limited afternoon hours, and were forbidden entrance to parks, theaters, pools, restaurants, cinemas, markets, fairs, museums, libraries, historical monuments, sporting events, and campgrounds. Jews were banned from all except the last car on public trains and buses. Synagogues, ancient houses of worship, were bombed.

In July of 1942, 12,884 Jews in Paris were arrested. More than 7,000 people, including some 4,000 children, were packed into Vélodrome d'Hiver, the indoor stadium in Paris, where there was no water, no food, and only ten toilets. They were later deported to the concentration camp at Auschwitz, Poland. Of the 7,000 arrested, thirty people survived. By 1944, large rewards were offered for Jews in hiding, and many more Jews were seized. In one notorious incident, French police raided the Colonie des Enfants, a children's home, and deported forty-one children to Auschwitz. During the war years, more than 84,000 people in France were sent to death camps.

On June 12, 1944, the American president, Franklin Delano Roosevelt, told the United States Congress of his goal to bring a group of refugees from Europe to the United States. On August 3, 1944, the *Henry Gibbins* arrived in New York Harbor.

The Europeans on board ranged in age from a newborn infant to an eighty-year-old man. They spoke eighteen languages and came from fifteen countries. Most were Jewish, though some were Protestant, Catholic, and Greek Orthodox. Among them were actors, singers, writers, shoemakers, doctors, bookbinders, and musicians. They had lost everything; some came without even a pair of shoes. They had been robbed of the dearest things in life—not only homes, property, and jobs but also parents, grandparents, aunts, uncles, sons, and daughters.

The 22,000 people living in Oswego, New York, a town on the shore of Lake Ontario, found themselves hosting this group of displaced, dispossessed, and disoriented strangers. In 1944, Oswego was a town of small industries surrounded by farms and was then, as it is now, one of the snowiest places in the United States. Fort Ontario, eighty acres of buildings and fields, had been an army base, bordered by Lake Ontario on one side and fenced in by barbed wire on the others. The military use of the fort had recently been discontinued, and although not everyone in Oswego welcomed these strangers, most hoped that the influx would add to the prosperity of their town.

In receiving the refugees, the town became unique in the United States. Although more than a hundred thousand German prisoners of war spent time safely and without incident in the United States between 1941 and 1945, the 982 people who came to Fort Ontario were the only group of refugees brought to America by the government during World War II. Of the millions whose lives were ravaged by the murder and destruction of the war, they represented a minute fraction.

On May 7, 1945, the German forces surrendered to the Allies unconditionally. In late December, Harry S. Truman, who had become president after Roosevelt's death on April 12, 1945, recommended that the Fort Ontario "guests" be allowed to remain in the United States, in accordance with existing immigration laws.

Early one morning, busloads of the Fort Ontario refugees left the United States and crossed the Rainbow Bridge at Niagara Falls. In Canada, they were welcomed by the American consul and each was handed an American visa, which granted legal entry to the United States. In the days and weeks that followed, the Fort Ontario residents scattered across America, some to join relatives—each to create a new life.